When Rafferty walked into the bunkhouse that evening, the men were gathered around Jacey and the baby, paying both the homage they deserved

Rafferty watched from the fringes.

There was no denying it. Jacey and her daughter had brought joy to the bunkhouse, the sense that with the two of them there, it would feel like Christmas all year round. The only problem was how to get them to stay on Lost Mountain Ranch for more than just another week.

Because when they left—if they left—for good, he knew it was going to feel as if his heart was breaking all over again....

Dear Reader,

Christmas is a time of great emotion, and if you are very lucky, great joy. But what happens when all that matters to you is taken away and the yuletide season is not something you look forward to?

This is the dilemma facing rancher Rafferty Evans. As a child, he loved everything about the holidays. That's no longer the case. Thanksgiving and Christmas serve only to remind him of a tragic loss. His plan to survive the season? Work doubly hard and avoid all holiday celebrations—even if it means being dubbed a modern-day Ebenezer Scrooge.

At least, that's his plan until one dark and stormy November night, when Jacey Lambert finds herself stranded on Lost Mountain Ranch.

Despite an unexpected turn of events that has left her without a job or a place to call home, Jacey loves life. She loves the holidays. And most of all, she loves the child she is carrying inside her. Jacey knows there is always something to celebrate. And soon she decides that, with her help, Rafferty Evans will recapture his Christmas spirit and realize that, too.

This story, dear readers, is my gift to you. I hope you have a wonderful holiday season!

Best wishes,

Cathy Gillen Thacker

Cathy Gillen Thacker
A BABY IN THE BUNKHOUSE

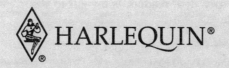

TORONTO • NEW YORK • LONDON
AMSTERDAM • PARIS • SYDNEY • HAMBURG
STOCKHOLM • ATHENS • TOKYO • MILAN • MADRID
PRAGUE • WARSAW • BUDAPEST • AUCKLAND

ISBN-13: 978-0-373-75241-6
ISBN-10:   0-373-75241-5

A BABY IN THE BUNKHOUSE

Copyright © 2008 by Cathy Gillen Thacker.

This edition published by arrangement with Harlequin Books S.A.

® and TM are trademarks of the publisher. Trademarks indicated with
® are registered in the United States Patent and Trademark Office, the
Canadian Trade Marks Office and in other countries.

www.eHarlequin.com

Printed in U.S.A.

ABOUT THE AUTHOR

Cathy Gillen Thacker is married and a mother of three. She and her husband spent eighteen years in Texas, and now reside in North Carolina. Her mysteries, romantic comedies and heartwarming family stories have made numerous appearances on bestseller lists, but her best reward, she says, is knowing one of her books made someone's day a little brighter. A popular Harlequin author for many years, she loves telling passionate stories with happy endings, and thinks nothing beats a good romance and a hot cup of tea! You can visit Cathy's Web site at www.cathygillenthacker.com for more information on her upcoming and previously published books, recipes and a list of her favorite things.

Books by Cathy Gillen Thacker

HARLEQUIN AMERICAN ROMANCE

  *The Brides of Holly Springs
**The McCabes: Next Generation
 †Texas Legacies: The Carrigans
††Made in Texas

Chapter One

"I figured I'd find you here, burning the midnight oil."

Rafferty Evans looked up from his computer screen to see his father standing in the doorway of the ranch-house study. At seventy-four, Eli Evans had finally agreed to retire. Which meant he had more time on his hands to stick his nose into his son's business. Sensing a talk coming on he'd rather avoid, Rafferty grumbled irritably, "Someone's got to do the books before the fall roundup starts."

Eli settled into a leather club chair. "The last two days of rain has you chomping at the bit."

Actually, Rafferty thought, he felt this way every November. Ignoring the flash of lightning outside, he went back to studying the numbers he'd been working on. "A lot to get done over the next six weeks."

Eli spoke over the deafening rumble of thunder. "Including the job of hiring a new bunkhouse cook."

"The hands chased away the last three with their incessant complaints. They can fend for themselves while I search for another."

"You know none of them can cook worth a darn."

"Then they should be more appreciative of anyone who has even a tiny bit of skill."

Eli thought about pursuing the matter, then evidently decided against it. "About Christmas…" he continued.

Rafferty stiffened. "I told you. I don't celebrate the holidays. Not anymore." *Not since the accident.*

Eli frowned with the quiet authority befitting a legendary Texas cattleman. "It's been two years."

Rafferty pushed back his chair and stood, hands shoved in the back pockets of his jeans. "I know how long it's been, Dad." He strode to the fireplace, picked up the poker and pushed the burning logs to the back of the grate. Sparks crackled from the embers.

"Life goes on," Eli continued.

"Holidays are for kids."

Eli fell silent.

Tired of being made to feel like Ebenezer Scrooge, Rafferty added another log to the fire, stalked to the window and looked out at the raging storm. Rain drummed on the roof. Another flash of lightning lit the sky—followed closely by a loud clap of thunder. Car headlights gleamed in the dark night and turned into the main gate.

Rafferty frowned and looked at the clock. It was midnight. He turned to his dad. "You expecting anyone?"

Eli shook his head. "Probably another tourist who lost his way."

Rafferty muttered a string of words not fit for mixed company. The car wasn't turning around. It was just sitting there, inside the ranch entrance, engine running.

His father came to stand beside him. "You want me to go out there, set 'em straight?"

Rafferty clapped a companionable hand on his dad's shoulder, and tried not to notice how frail it felt. He didn't know what he would do if he lost his dad, too. He pushed aside the troubling thought. "I'll do it," he said. Then ordered gently, "You go on to bed."

"Sure?"

Rafferty knew this kind of damp cold was hard on his father's arthritis. He shook his head. "I'm sure they're just turned around. I'll make sure they get back to the main road."

"The news said the river's rising," Eli warned.

Rafferty grabbed his slicker and hat from the coatrack in the hall. Shrugging on both, he swung open the front door and stepped out onto the porch. The chill air and the fresh green scent of rain were invigorating. "I won't waste any time making sure they get on their way."

OF ALL THE THINGS Jacey Lambert had expected to happen to her today, coming to the end of the road was not one of them. But after miles of traversing an increasingly rough and narrow highway that had dead-ended into the entrance of the Lost Mountain Ranch, that was exactly where she was.

She had gotten completely turned around.

She was tired and hungry. Her car was low on fuel.

Worst of all, her cell phone hadn't worked for miles.

Would it be rude to knock on the door of the sprawling adobe ranch house just ahead?

Before she could formulate an answer, she heard the sound of an engine starting.

She looked up to see a pickup truck headed her way. It stopped just short of her Volvo station wagon.

A cowboy in a black hat and a yellow rain slicker climbed out of the cab, strode purposefully over to the driver's side.

As he neared her, Jacey's mouth went dry.

It wasn't so much the size of him that caught her off guard. Although she guessed he was six foot three or so—with broad shoulders and the long-legged, impressively muscled physique of a man who made his living roping calves…or whatever it was cowboys did.

It was the face beneath the brim of that hat that truly made her catch her breath. Ruggedly handsome, with even features, a straight nose, arresting blue eyes and walnut-brown hair peeking out from under his cowboy hat. He was clean-shaven, a plus in her estimation. Jacey hated a man with a scraggly beard.

And she was digressing.

He'd obviously said something as she was sliding down her window, and he was waiting for her to answer. Which would have been okay if she'd known the question.

She swallowed to add moisture to her parched throat. "What did you say?" she asked.

"This is private property. You're trespassing," he repeated, clearly not all that happy about being pulled out in the torrential rain to deal with an interloper.

So much for the renowned West Texas hospitality, she thought on a sigh.

She indicated the highway map she had spread across her steering wheel—the one that covered her unusual girth. "I'm lost."

His eyes narrowed. "I figured."

"I'm trying to find Indian Lodge at Davis Mountains State Park."

He angled a thumb in the opposite direction. Then growled, "You're at least sixty miles of back roads from there."

Which might as well have been six hundred, given how low visibility was in this pouring rain and thick mist. Even in good conditions, the speed limit on these winding mountain roads was barely thirty-five miles per hour.

These weren't good conditions.

Plus, her back was aching, and all she wanted was a good bed and a soft pillow.

So much for her plan to do a little leisurely sightseeing on the way to her sister's place in El Paso. "How far to the nearest hotel then?" Jacey asked, more than ready to be en route again.

"About the same," he told her grimly.

She suppressed a groan. "Can you give me directions?"

He shook his head. "Too difficult to follow, even without the bad weather. I'll lead you back to the main highway, point you in the right direction, and you can take it from there."

Telling herself she could make it another hour or two if she had to, Jacey smiled with gratitude. "Thanks."

She put her road map aside while the sexy cowboy in the yellow rain slicker stalked back to his pickup. He motioned for her to back out of the gate, then climbed into the cab of his truck. She did as directed and he took the lead.

Body still aching all over from way more hours in the car than she'd expected, Jacey turned her windshield wipers on high and followed the large pickup in front of her. They'd gone roughly two miles down the paved lane, when he started down a hill, then braked so abruptly she almost slid right into him. Wondering what the holdup was, she waited as the rain came down even harder.

She didn't have long to wait. He put his truck in Park, hopped out and strode back to the driver side of her station wagon once again. "There's water on the bridge," he shouted through the window.

Jacey's view of the low stone bridge was obscured. "How much?" she shouted back.

He grimaced. "About a foot."

Jacey swore heatedly. If she drove across the low-water crossing, she'd be swept off the concrete bridge and into the current of the river. She looked at him, heart pounding. "Now what?"

"There's a ditch on either side of the lane, and no room to turn around. You're going to have to back up the hill."

Jacey was not good at backing up. Never mind in these conditions. "Can't I just—"

"Just do it," he said abruptly. "And stay off the berm."

"Easier said than done," Jacey muttered as she took her car out of Park and put it in Reverse.

For one thing, she didn't have headlights behind her, which meant she was essentially backing up in the dark. For another, the road wasn't a perfectly straight line. In addition, she couldn't recall exactly where the curve at the top of the steep hill began. And last but not least she wasn't as physically agile these days as she normally was. Which made turning around to look over her shoulder while still steering with one hand very technically difficult, if not damn near impossible.

So it was really no surprise when she felt the station-wagon wheels on the right side slip as she inadvertently left the paved surface and hit the gravel along the edge. Slowing even more, she turned the steering wheel in the opposite direction in an effort to get back up on the road.

To no avail. The heavy rains, combined with the mud, had the wheels on the right side of the car sinking even lower. Jacey stopped what she was doing, not sure how to proceed.

The cowboy got out of his truck.

He stalked back, took a look and muttered a string of words she was just as happy not to catch.

"You're not stuck. Yet," he said.

Thank heaven for small miracles. Jacey flashed a weak smile.

"Just give it a little bit of gas and keep backing up slowly," he instructed.

Jacey put her foot on the accelerator, pressed ever so lightly. The car didn't move—at all.

He frowned. "More than that."

Jacey pressed down harder. The wheels spun and the right side of her car sunk. She was stuck. Stuck in the mud on a lonely country road in Texas with a disgruntled cowpuncher staring at her as if he wanted to be anywhere else on earth.

She knew exactly how he felt.

Exhaling ferociously, he strode back to her side, while lightning flashed overhead. He stomped around to further examine the wheels on her tilting car then came back. "We're not going to be able to get your vehicle out until morning," he said as another clap of thunder split the air.

Jacey had been afraid of that.

"We can put you up in the bunkhouse."

She blinked. This whole night was getting more and more bizarre. "With…*cowboys?*" she echoed incredulously.

"The cook's quarters are unoccupied right now," he told her curtly. "And they're private."

Jacey faltered. Asking someone she didn't know for directions was one thing, accepting lodging another. "I don't know…"

The cowboy seemed to have no such reservations. "What choice do you have? Besides sleeping in the car?"

And they could both see, with the most necessary belongings of her life taking up every available inch of space in the car, there was definitely no room for that.

It was only as Jacey was grabbing her purse and the small overnight bag she had planned to take with her into the lodge that she realized he hadn't told her his name.

As soon as she got her bearings after working her way out of the car, she thrust out her hand. "I'm Jacey Lambert," she said with a smile.

He reached out to swallow her palm in a warm, strong grip, and his gaze fell to her rounded belly. His polite but remote smile faded. "You're pregnant."

"You just now noticed?" Jacey was approximately two weeks away from actually delivering her baby. She felt large as a cow.

Irritation tautened his lips. "I wasn't looking."

"Guess not."

They stared at each other in the pouring rain.

He had a rain slicker on. She did not. And the water pouring down from the heavens was quickly drenching her hair and clothing.

Evidently realizing that, at long last, he put an arm around her shoulders and hustled her toward his truck.

"I hope you're better at backing up a vehicle than I was," she joked as he shifted his large capable hands to her waist and lifted her into the cab.

He shot her a level look, a grimness that seemed to go soul deep in his eyes.

"I don't think I'll have any problem," he said as he climbed behind the wheel.

"You still haven't told me your name," Jacey said after he successfully steered the truck past her car, and they proceeded rapidly toward the entrance of Lost Mountain Ranch.

"Rafferty Evans."

"Nice to meet you, Rafferty."

Her greeting was met with silence.

His mood was even more remote as he parked at a group of sprawling adobe buildings. They got out and walked the short distance across the pavement in the pouring rain—this time beneath a wide umbrella he'd plucked from behind the driver's seat. When they reached the portal of the bunkhouse, he shook the umbrella out, closed it and set it just beside the door.

Looking over at her, he said, "The hired hands are asleep. So if you could be as quiet as possible…"

She nodded, incredibly grateful now that safety was upon her. She didn't care if this handsome stranger had wanted to rescue her and her unborn child or not—he had.

"No problem," she told him just as quietly.

The bunkhouse was a large, square building, built in the same pueblo style as the main ranch house.

He held the front door for her and motioned her inside. She walked into a spacious great room, with a long wooden table and chairs on one side, a huge stone hearth in the middle— with a dying fire—and a grouping of overstuffed chairs, sofa and large-screen television on the other side. There were three closed doors on each side of the large gathering room that looked like the entrance to private bedrooms or quarters. All was dark and quiet.

"Kitchen's to the rear if you need anything. Help yourself," Rafferty Evans leaned down to whisper in her ear.

Taking her by the elbow, he guided her toward a door. Just as she had suspected, it opened onto a nice-size bedroom, with dresser, chair and private bath. A stack of clean linens sat on the end of the unmade bed.

"I'll see you first thing tomorrow morning," he said.

Then he turned on his heel and left.

ELI WAS WAITING for Rafferty when he walked back in the ranch house. "Get everything all taken care of?"

Rafferty exhaled, not surprised his dad had not gone on to bed, as directed.

He hung his wet hat and slicker on one of the hooks on the wall and stalked into the kitchen. "Not exactly." He got a beer out of the fridge, twisted off the cap and flipped it into the trash.

He took a long pull of the golden brew before continuing, "The bridge is underwater—which, thanks to the fog, we weren't able to see until we got right up on it. When we were backing up, the woman got her car stuck in the mud, so we'll have that to look forward to in the morning."

Eli paused to take this all in. "Where is she?" he asked eventually, brows furrowing.

As far away from me as possible under the circumstances.

Rafferty took another pull on his beer, trying not to think how incredibly beautiful the woman was. "Cook's quarters in the bunkhouse."

Eli did a double take and surveyed his son with a critical eye. "You put a *lady* in the bunkhouse?"

Worse than that, Rafferty thought, he put a *pregnant* lady in there.

Figuring his father didn't need to know that part of the equation yet, Rafferty shrugged and ambled back to the fridge. He rummaged around for something to eat, trying hard not to think of Jacey Lambert's ripe madonna-like figure and drenched state.

The bunkhouse was plenty warm. She had two blankets, a stack of sheets and towels, a warm shower if she wanted it and an overnight case that undoubtedly held dry clothing. There was no reason for him to worry. She'd be fine. If she wasn't, well, he had no doubt she was just as capable at calling for help and waking all the cowboys up as she had been backing her car into the ditch. They'd let him know. In the meantime, he needed to put her and everything else he still preferred not to think about, out of his mind.

"She seemed okay with it," Rafferty said. Deciding he needed some food in his stomach, too, he grabbed a slice of precut cheddar.

"That's not how we do things around here," Eli reprimanded in his low, gravelly voice.

Didn't he know it. Rafferty downed his snack, and another quarter of his beverage. Avoiding his dad's look, he walked over to the recycling bin. "Look. She was dead tired—she's probably already asleep." He dropped the empty bottle into the plastic bin. "Which is what I plan to do." Go to bed. Forget everything.

"We're going to talk about this in the morning," Eli warned.

Rafferty imagined they would. But not now. Not when he had so many unwanted memories trying to crowd their way back in.

"'Night, Dad." Rafferty gave his dad a brief, one-armed hug and headed down the hall that ran the length of the seven-thousand-square-foot ranch house.

It was only when he reached his room that the loss hit him like a fist in the center of his chest.

But instead of the image of his own family in his mind's eye, as he stripped down to his T-shirt and boxers and went to brush his teeth, he saw the trespasser he had encountered in the pouring rain.

She had glossy brown hair, a shade or two darker than his, that framed her face with sexy bangs and fell around her slender shoulders like a dark silky cloud. If only her allure had ended there, he thought resentfully. It hadn't. He'd been held captive by a lively gaze, framed with thick lashes and dark expressive brows.

Everything about the woman, from the feisty set of her chin and the fact she was stranded late at night, pregnant and alone, to the way she carried herself, said she was independent past the point of all common sense.

Thank God she'd be leaving in the morning, as soon as he could get her station wagon out of the muck, Rafferty thought as he got into bed.

The sooner she left, the sooner he could stop thinking about Jacey Lambert's merry smile and soft green eyes.

Now all it had to do was stop raining.

Chapter Two

Jacey woke at dawn, her body aching the way it always did when she'd spent too long behind the wheel of a car, her stomach rumbling with hunger.

She opened her eyes, and for a second as she looked around the rustically appointed room, she had trouble recalling where she was.

Then she remembered the rain—which was still pounding torrentially on the roof overhead—the jagged slash of lightning across the dark night sky, thunder so loud it shook the ground beneath her. And a man in a black hat and a long yellow rain slicker coming to her rescue.

Jacey closed her eyes against the image of that ruggedly handsome face and tall, muscular frame.

She didn't know what it was about Rafferty Evans. She'd seen plenty of men with soft, touchable brown hair and stunning blue eyes. Taken item by item, there'd been nothing all that remarkable about his straight nose and even features. So what if every inch of him had been unerringly masculine and he'd been six foot three inches of strength and confidence? Just because his shoulders and chest had looked broad enough to shelter her from even the fiercest storm was no reason to tingle all over just remembering the sight of him, or the gentle, deferential way he'd helped her out of her car.

But she was. And that, Jacey decided, was not good.

She had a Volvo station wagon that was still stuck in the mud. And a baby inside her needing nourishment.

Padding barefoot to the private bathroom where she'd taken a warm shower the evening before, she slipped inside and began to dress in the long, pine-green maternity skirt and cream-colored sweater. Needing to feel a lot more put together than she had the evening before, she took the time to apply makeup and sweep her hair into a bouncy ponytail high on the back of her head.

She slipped her feet back into a pair of soft brown leather stack-heeled shoes that were going to be woefully inadequate for the conditions and repacked her overnight case. Leaving it on the bed for the moment, she opened the door to the main cabin of the bunkhouse and stared at what she saw.

Five genuine cowpunchers of varying sizes and ages, all staring at her. Waiting, it seemed. "Hi. I'm Jacey Lambert." Awkwardly, she held out her hand.

The beanpole-thin cowpoke who was nearly seven feet tall was first to clasp her hand. "Stretch."

Jacey could see why he was named that.

"I'm Curly." A mid-twentyish man with golden curls and bedroom eyes was second in line.

Obviously, Jacey thought, as they clasped palms a bit too long, he was the self-proclaimed lady-killer of the bunch.

"Everyone calls me Red," said a third.

The youngest cowhand couldn't have been more than nineteen, Jacey figured, and had bright red hair and freckles.

"I'm Hoss," said a big fellow with a round belly and a receding hairline.

So named because of his striking resemblance, Jacey figured, to a character on the old *Bonanza* television show that still played on cable in Texas.

"And I'm Gabby," said the last.

Jacey estimated the forty-something man's scraggly beard to be at least five days old, if not more.

"We are so glad to see you," Gabby continued, pumping Jacey's hand enthusiastically.

"Yeah, after what happened with Biscuits, we didn't think we were going to get anyone else in here, but we're starving."

"Actually," Jacey said, not sure what they were talking about, "so am I."

"We, uh, know you just got here," Stretch said, patting his concave belly, "but could you take mercy on us and cook us some breakfast?"

Jacey blinked. "Right now?"

"Yeah." The group shrugged in consensus. "If you wouldn't mind."

Jacey figured she had to repay the ranch's hospitality somehow. "Sure." She smiled. "I'd be glad to."

HOPING AGAINST WHAT he knew the situation likely to be, Rafferty nixed a visit to the bunkhouse—where their unexpected guest was likely still sleeping the morning away—and drove down to the river. Or as close as he could get to the low water crossing; the concrete bridge was now buried under several feet of fast-moving water. With the rain still pouring down there was no way it would recede. Not until the precipitation stopped, and even then, probably not for another twenty-four to thirty-six hours.

Realizing what this meant, Rafferty stomped back to his pickup. En route back to the ranch he passed the red station wagon. It was still half off the berm of the lonely dead-end road that led to the ranch, its right wheels buried up past the hubcaps in the muddy ditch.

Worse, it looked as if it was packed to the gills with everything from clothes to kitchenware to what appeared to be a baby stroller and infant car seat. They'd have an easier time getting the vehicle out of the mud if it weren't so weighted down with belongings, but the thought of having to unpack all those belongings, only to repack them again made him scowl all the more.

He and the men couldn't start the fall roundup until the rain stopped.

Knowing however there were some things that could be done—like getting that car out of the mud so their uninvited visitor could be out of their way as soon as possible—Rafferty drove toward the bunkhouse.

He was pleased to see the lights on, the men up.

Pausing only long enough to shake the water off his slicker, he strode on in, then stopped in his tracks. Stretch was setting the table. Curly was pouring coffee. Red, Gabby and Hoss were carrying platters of food. Steaming-hot, delicious-smelling, food. The likes of which they hadn't been blessed with since he couldn't remember when.

In the middle of it all was Jacey Lambert.

Impossibly, she looked even prettier than she had the night before, her cheeks all flushed—whether from the heat of the stove or the thoroughly smitten glances of the men all around her—he couldn't tell.

"Hey, boss," Stretch said.

"I'll get you a plate." Red rushed to comply.

"Man, this stuff smells good." Hoss moved to hold out a chair for Jacey at the head of the table.

Flushing all the more, she murmured her thanks and

slipped into the seat with as much grace as the baby bump on her slender frame would allow.

Rafferty felt a stirring inside him. He pushed it away.

"We didn't think we were going to get someone to cook for us again until, well, heck, who knows when," Curly said, helping himself to a generous serving of scrambled eggs laced with tortilla strips, peppers and cheddar cheese.

Curly handed the bowl of migas to Jacey, while the others ladled fried potatoes, biscuits and cooked cinnamon apples onto their plates.

Gabby paused long enough to say grace. Then the eating commenced in earnest.

To Rafferty's chagrin, the food was every bit as delicious as it looked, and then some. From his position at the opposite end of the table, he gazed curiously at Jacey. "You're a chef by profession?"

Her vibrant green eyes locked with his and she shook her head. "Property manager. Er…I was." She lifted a staying hand, correcting, "I'm not now. Although I *like* to cook…"

"I can see why," Gabby interjected cheerfully. "You're dang good at it."

"Thank you."

"Which is why we're so glad you're here," Stretch added.

Rafferty could tell by the relaxed smile on her face that Jacey Lambert had no idea what the men were talking about. He, however, did. Which left him to deliver the bad news. "She's not our cook," he said.

Uncomprehending expressions all around.

He swore silently and tried again. "I haven't hired her. She's not working here."

"Then what's she doing sleeping in our bunkhouse?" Hoss demanded, upset.

"My station wagon got stuck in the mud last night," Jacey said. She leaned back in her chair slightly, rubbing a gentle, protective hand across her belly.

Turning his attention away from her pregnancy and the unwanted memories it evoked, Rafferty looked at the men. "She'll be on her way to wherever she was headed—"

"Indian Lodge, in the Davis Mountains State Park and then El Paso," Jacey informed them with a smile.

"—as soon as the river goes down."

"Then let's hope it never goes down," Curly joshed with a seductive wink aimed her way.

Everyone laughed—including Jacey—everyone except Rafferty. Finished with his breakfast, he stood. He was about to start issuing orders, when Jacey let out a soft, anguished cry.

All eyes went to her.

She blew out a quick, jerky breath. The color drained from her face, then flooded right back in.

"You okay?" every man there asked in unison.

Jacey pushed back her chair, got clumsily to her feet. Trembling, she looked down at the puddle on the seat of her chair. Eyes wide, she whispered, "I think my water just broke!"

THIS CAN'T BE HAPPENING! Jacey thought as the door to the bunkhouse opened once again and a silver-haired, older man who bore the same rugged features Rafferty Evans sported walked in. Eyes immediately going to her, he swept off his rain-drenched hat and held it against his chest. "What's going on?" he asked with the quiet authority of someone who had long owned the place.

Jacey braced herself with a hand to the table. "I think…I'm having my baby," she said as a hard pain gripped her, causing her to double over in pain.

The ache spreading across her middle was so hard and intense, she couldn't help but moan.

Her knees began to buckle.

The next thing she knew, Rafferty was at her side. One hand around her spine, the other beneath her knees, her swept her up off her feet and carried her the short distance to the bed where she'd spent the night.

He laid her down gently.

Jacey shut her eyes against the continuing vise across her middle.

"We need to get you to the hospital," Rafferty said gruffly.

Another pain gripped her, worse than the first. She grabbed Rafferty Evans's arm and held on tight, increasing her hold as the knifelike intensity built. The combination of panic and pain built; hot tears gathered behind her eyes. *Oh, God.* "I don't think I can wait for an ambulance." Glad she was lying down—she surely would have collapsed had she been on her feet—she blew out another burst of quick, jerky breaths.

This was not something Rafferty wanted to hear. He stared down at her, willing her to stop the labor, as surely as he had rescued her the night before. "Yes. You can."

Hysterical laughter bubbled up in her throat. She shook her head and tightened her hold on him before he could exit the cook's quarters. "I can feel the baby coming!"

"It's still going to take a while."

Was it? She blew out more air, beginning to feel even more frantic now. This wasn't supposed to happen for another two weeks!

The group of cowhands pushed their way in. Along with them was the elder rancher. "I just called the hospital," he reported grimly. "The Medevac chopper can't take off until the fog lifts, which won't be for at least another half hour. And with the bridge out… If this baby's in a hurry, we may have to deliver it ourselves."

Jacey couldn't help it—she uttered an anguished cry as another excruciating pain circled her waist, pushing downward.

Vaguely she was aware of Rafferty swearing.

"Don't look at us!" the group of cowboys said, already backing up, palms raised in surrender. "None of us know anything about birthing babies."

The elder rancher looked at Rafferty. "Looks like you're on, son."

Rafferty did a double take that was no more encouraging. "Why me?" he demanded.

"Because you're the only one of us who's had any veterinary training!" Stretch said.

Veterinary training! Jacey thought.

Rafferty looked as unimpressed by his education as Jacey. "One semester," he stated plainly, glaring at the hired hands who circled the bed. "That hardly qualifies me to work as an obstetrician."

"Maybe not," Hoss drawled, "but right now, boss, you're all we got."

Besieged with another contraction, Jacey grabbed the blanket she was lying on with both fists. This was going to be some story. First, she got hopelessly lost, something she never did. Then she drove her car into a ditch, spent the night in a bunkhouse, was unwittingly mistaken for the new cook, whipped up breakfast to great acclaim…and then went into hard, fast labor. Next thing she knew… She moaned out loud as the pain increased unbearably. "I can't believe I'm talking about having my baby delivered by a vet-school dropout!"

"Now, now. He's got to know something," Curly soothed with a wink.

"Yeah, he delivers all the horses and cows on the ranch," Red added helpfully. "The ones that need help birthing anyway."

"It's not the same thing," Rafferty protested grimly.

"Not even close," Jacey agreed in the same humorless tone.

"Close enough," the older man countered sagely, stepping in with that cool air of authority once again. "Emergency Medical Services said the docs over at the Summit Hospital E.R. will answer any questions you have and talk you through it until they can get here—just give 'em a call." He pushed the phone into Rafferty's hand, then extended his palm to Jacey. "I'm Eli Evans by the way," he said warmly, reassuring her with a glance that all would be well. "My son and I own this place."

Eli seemed like a nice guy. Hospitable and ready to lend a hand, unlike his son, who seemed to be offering aid with as much reluctance as Jacey felt receiving it.

Another contraction wrapped around her middle. It was all Jacey could do not to whimper as the pain increased. Recalling her labor coach's advice to relax and distract herself from the discomfort as much as possible during the early stage of labor, Jacey puffed, "Nice to meet you, sir."

Her know-it-all sister had been right—Jacey shouldn't have taken her sweet old time getting to El Paso for the birth.

Jacey forced a determined smile and kept her attention on Eli. "And thanks for the lodging last night."

"You're welcome." Eli squeezed her hand reassuringly, before releasing it. "Although, for the record," he said mildly, "I would have put you up in the ranch house."

"My room was fine." She'd slept well. Which was good, considering what she had ahead of her.

"You ought to taste the breakfast she cooked us," Stretch remarked.

Eli's craggy brow lifted in surprise. "You cooked?"

Jacey shrugged as perspiration beaded her entire body. "It seemed a fair trade. Besides, we were all hungry."

Unable to help herself as the pain increased to defcon levels, she let out a low, keening moan.

Every cowboy in the room—except Rafferty—stepped away from the bed she was lying on. As if it would somehow help to give her space.

And maybe it would, Jacey thought as sweat dampened her hair and heat pushed up her neck into her face. Despite the fact she was now once again diligently doing her Lamaze breathing, she felt as if she would never be able to get enough air.

Father and son exchanged concerned glances she wished she hadn't seen. "Let us know if you need anything." Eli directed the cowboys out, and the door shut behind them.

Jacey and Rafferty were alone, and Rafferty looked about as happy with the situation as she was.

He punched in a number, stated he was going to be the one delivering the baby, then listened intently. "This your first baby?" he asked Jacey.

"Yes."

"Then we're probably going to have plenty of time."

Rafferty went back to talking on the phone, absorbed what sounded like a slew of in-case-things-do-get-out-of-hand instructions. Promising to call back if he needed further instructions, he hung up and opened the bedroom door. "Get me a stack of clean towels and something to wrap the baby in!" he called.

The cowboys milling nervously about jumped to attention. Mere seconds later clean linens were shoved into Rafferty's arms.

"Boil a pair of scissors and some string. I want 'em sterile," he barked before shutting the door and striding back to the narrow twin bed. Despite his lack of experience, he carried himself with a gunslinger's confidence, which, oddly enough, made her want to kick him in the shin. Perverse as it might be, she wanted him to feel as panicked and out of control as she did. She wanted them to be on a level playing field.

A glint of humor in his blue eyes, he surveyed her mussed hair and flushed cheeks. "Want a bullet to bite on?"

"Very funny," she panted.

"Whiskey to kill the pain?"

"You're a laugh riot." Tears streamed down her face. "All those wonderful delivery-room drugs would probably help just about now."

"I'm sure they'll give you a shot of whatever as soon as the EMS gets here. Meanwhile—" he dragged the ladder-back chair over to the end of the bed "—we're going to have to get you better situated." He patted the end of the mattress. "So you're going to have to scoot down to the end."

With her whole body wrapped in a vise? Suddenly, she was trembling from head to toe. "I don't th-th-think I c-can."

"I'll help you." Gentle, reassuring now, he put his warm, strong hands beneath her, then shifted her bottom to the end of the mattress. He slipped onto the seat of the chair, positioning her legs so her knees were raised, her feet flat on the mattress. He lifted her again, held her there with one hand and spread two clean towels out beneath her.

Another wave of intense pressure rocked Jacey's frame. Was it her imagination or could she literally feel the baby bump moving lower…? "I know it doesn't seem possible… but I r-r-really think I f-f-f-eel the head."

"Only one way to find out." He was so calm and matter-of-fact they might have been talking about the weather. "We'll take a look, see how far your cervix is dilated."

"Guess those veterinary classes are coming in handy."

"Now who's the smart-ass?"

Grinning, she had a feeling he'd be a fun guy to spar with. Under other circumstances... She sucked in a breath as another contraction gripped her.

The look on his face as he checked out the situation confirmed her worst suspicions and the reason for her distress. "You need to call for help again?"

All business, Rafferty shook his head. "No time."

No time?

"Hang in there, Jacey." His voice was as warm as his touch. "We can do this."

Suddenly, with him by her side...she felt as if they could.

He remained focused on the task ahead. "I'm going to have to touch you." He applied a very gentle counterpressure to her perineum that made her feel as though things were getting back into control, however slightly. "And you're going to need to pant or blow through the contractions. Just don't push. Not yet. I'll tell you when."

Marshaling every bit of self-control she had, she fought through the excruciating pain and did as instructed.

"I can see the head. It's coming out...nice and slow...which is good. We don't want to rush anything. Wait! I've got to unhook this loop of umbilical cord from around the baby's neck."

Jacey sucked in a breath and went as still as possible, not even daring to breathe.

"Easy does it," he murmured as he gently worked the cord over the baby's head. "Okay, we're good to go," he said with a smile. She felt the backs of Rafferty's hands brush against her spread thighs as he took the baby's head in both his palms. "Now push! We've got a shoulder...an upper arm....! Another shoulder and...a baby!" he declared triumphantly.

Jacey felt a whoosh as the infant slipped completely free of her body. Another rush of fluid. Incredibly happy and at peace, she watched as Rafferty cleared the mouth of mucus and held the squirming, squalling baby aloft so she could see.

A LUMP CLOGGED Rafferty's throat as the baby let out one lusty cry after another. A cheer went up on the other side of the door that paired nicely with Jacey's exultant cry as she met her infant daughter for the first time. "Hello, Caitlin, my sweet baby girl," she whispered, happy tears streaming down her face.

"Congratulations," he said gruffly, pushing aside memories of another place, another time and life that had been cruelly taken away.

He wrapped the pink, squalling baby in a towel and handed Caitlin to her mother.

Too overwhelmed to do more than nod, tears of joy streaming down her face, Jacey cradled the newborn close to her chest. Forcing himself to rein in the feelings that threatened to overwhelm him, too, Rafferty returned to the end of the bed and concentrated on the task still at hand. Tears pricked the back of his eyes. Determinedly, he willed them away. "Anyone you want to call?" he asked in the most impersonal tone he could manage.

Abruptly, Jacey went very still. "If you're asking about a…husband…"

He was.

As reluctant as he was to imagine her with any other guy, he didn't want her to be alone, either.

"I don't have one."

Rafferty should have figured that would be the case, given how independent she was. He checked, saw the afterbirth still attached to the umbilical cord, well on its way.

He went to the door. Got the sterilized scissors and string from the cowboys on the other side. Shut it again. "Baby daddy then," he prompted.

Blissfully entranced with the quieting bundle in her arms, Jacey shook her head, replied softly, "Don't have one of those either."

Rafferty checked out her left hand. Sure enough, it bore no wedding ring.

Which meant what? The baby's father had abandoned her? Died? Was around but chose not to be involved? Her expression gave no clue. And in fact, she seemed defiantly determined not to discuss it with him.

He figured that was her right. He didn't want to talk about his personal life, either. Still, there had to be somebody who cared, someone to notify.

"Family then," he insisted matter-of-factly. With the placenta out, Rafferty was free to tie off and then cut the umbilical cord. Finished, he tucked the towel in around the baby once again, keeping the newborn warm.

"I've got a sister in El Paso who was supposed to be my labor-and-delivery coach. I'll call her after we get to the hospital."

Without warning, there was a *thump thump thump* of an approaching chopper.

"Sounds like the Medevac team is here," Rafferty said.

Given the heart-wrenching memories that this experience had conjured up, it wasn't a moment too soon.

Chapter Three

"Heard you and the baby were about to be released." Eli Evans stood in the doorway of Jacey's hospital room two days later. Hat held against his chest, he asked, "Mind if I come in?"

Jacey smiled. "Please do. I owe you and your son and everyone at the ranch so much." For the food and lodging, getting her car out of the mud, and most especially, for delivering her baby.

Not that she'd seen or heard a word from the vet-school dropout who'd done the honors since the EMS had rushed into the bunkhouse and taken over.

The sexy rancher hadn't called. Hadn't come by. Or sent flowers.

And while technically she knew there was no reason Rafferty Evans should have, she'd privately hoped she would see him again. She thought they'd bonded during Caitlin's birth, the way strangers who lived through an unexpected trauma together did.

Obviously not.

Rafferty wasn't going to be around to see her through the transition into motherhood. He wasn't going to help her ward off her overbearing older sister, Mindy, or be there to lean on in the days ahead. Even though for one brief, fanciful moment, Jacey had wished that were the case....

Oblivious to her thoughts, Eli set a glass vase of flowers down on the table beside her hospital bed.

"As far as the men are concerned, it's the other way around," Eli told her. "They haven't stopped talking about that breakfast you made them."

Happy to be drawn back to reality, Jacey waved off the praise. "It was no big deal."

"To a bunch of hired hands who haven't had a decent meal in months, it is. Which is why I'm here." Eli paused to gently touch Caitlin's cheek in the same way a loving grandfather might, then dropped his weather-beaten hand and stepped back. "I promised 'em I'd at least ask if you wanted a job as ranch cook."

Jacey blinked. Talk about providence! Loving the soft, sweet smell of baby, she held Caitlin closer to her chest. "You're kidding."

Eli sobered. "No, Ms. Lambert, I surely am not. We've got fall roundup going on out there for the next five or six weeks. And seven men in need of three square meals a day. I understand you just had a baby and have got to have some time to recuperate. That you probably have a job elsewhere."

So he'd heard she had no husband to support her. That meant Rafferty had told him. Did Rafferty and his father also guess her options at the moment were severely limited, thanks to the unexpected loss of her job in San Antonio the previous week?

No matter. Without warning, she'd found herself in need of new employment and a new apartment, since her previous place had come with the job. Unless she wanted to impose on her sister indefinitely. And Jacey really didn't, given the unending stream of advice the terminally overprotective Mindy would no doubt be handing out on a daily, hourly basis. She had no other options at the moment. But this.

"Actually," Jacey cut in cheerfully, "I'm looking for employment as well as a place to live—temporarily anyway." She couldn't say she'd want to live in such isolation indefinitely. But right now it wouldn't be a bad place to be while she figured out her options and looked for another position in her regular line of work.

Eli worked the brim of his Stetson hat in his age-spotted hands. "Any way you could do this for us? We'd make it worth your while."

To Jacey's shock, Eli named a salary on par with what she had been earning with the management company.

Joy bubbled up inside her. "I could keep Caitlin with me at all times?"

"Absolutely. We'd see you had everything the two of you need."

We. Abruptly remembering the Lost Mountain Ranch was jointly owned and operated, Jacey bit her lower lip. "What about your son? How is Rafferty going to feel about this?" Initially, he hadn't wanted her on their property at all.

Eli regarded Jacey with a look that told the new mom that her instincts were right—her presence as ranch cook wasn't something Rafferty would desire.

"You leave that to me," Eli said.

"I DON'T CARE how providential it seems. Taking the job as the Lost Mountain Ranch bunkhouse cook is a mistake," Mindy told Jacey as she dressed her baby girl in her pink-and-white going-home-from-the-hospital outfit. "Because you know exactly what's going to happen."

Jacey wrapped Caitlin in a matching baby blanket. "I'll save money for a fresh start?"

Mindy swept a hand through her cropped brown hair and turned her laser-sharp brown eyes to Jacey. "You'll get too comfortable. Before you know it, you'll be settling for what's convenient and easy again, rather than holding out for what you really want."

Jacey handed Caitlin over to her older sister. As always, Mindy was nicely dressed, in an elegantly tailored shirt and slacks. "Look, I know you love me…" she began.

Mindy cuddled her niece with familial love and tenderness. "And Caitlin, too."

"And want only the best for me," Jacey continued, wishing her big sis were a lot less protective, now that they were both grown-up and headed down different paths.

Mindy exhaled, exasperated. "I'm just telling you what Mom would have said if she were here."

Their late mother, Jacey was fairly certain, would have understood. After all, Karol Lambert had made her own share of sacrifices as she struggled to support herself and two small daughters after her husband died.

But figuring it would do no good to say that to Mindy—who had reacted to their beloved mother's death, when Mindy was nineteen and Jacey was eighteen, by focusing solely on setting goals and achieving them—Jacey kept quiet. Instead, she slipped into the adjoining bath to put on the gray and pink warm-ups she intended to wear.

"You need to call Cash, tell him you and the baby are in trouble," Mindy said.

Eager for the time she'd actually be able to go out and run again, Jacey put on her socks and athletic shoes. Finished, she marched back out to confront her sister. "First of all, I'm thirty-one years old. I can make my own decisions. Second, I don't have a clue where Cash is. And third, you know very well that he doesn't want to be involved."

Mindy frowned. "Caitlin is his baby!"

Jacey exhaled slowly and counted backward from ten. "Not in any way that counts," she argued.

Mindy's jaw dropped.

Wondering why her sister was so flummoxed—certainly not from the same old disagreement they'd been over countless times in the last nine months—Jacey pivoted in the direction of Mindy's gaze. Suddenly, she understood. Rafferty Evans was standing in the doorway, bigger than life. Her eyes drifted over him as shock set in. She thought he had looked good rescuing her and delivering her baby. It was nothing compared to the way he looked this afternoon in a dark brown leather jacket, light blue shirt and jeans. His thick brown hair had been cut since she'd seen him last. The clean, rumpled strands were an inch and a half in length, slightly wavy.

"Well, this explains part of it anyway," Mindy drawled.

Figuring it would do no good to tell her sister the situation wasn't what it seemed, Jacey turned her attention to Rafferty.

Reassuring herself she was immune to his studly presence, she demanded, "What are you doing here?"

His mesmerizing eyes kept more private than they revealed. "I heard you needed a ride back to the ranch."

Her heart beat rapidly for no particular reason. "Your father said he was going to do it."

He sauntered in, the fragrance of soap and man clinging to his clean-shaven jaw. "That was when your projected release time was this morning." Steering well clear of Mindy and the baby, he lounged against the wall and shrugged his broad shoulders. "When it turned out to be later, I got tapped.

He had an appointment with his rheumatologist in Fort Stockton this afternoon, although he'll probably be back at the ranch by the time we get there."

"Oh."

Mindy handed Caitlin back to Jacey. As soon as the transfer was accomplished, she made a beeline for Rafferty and shook his hand with the intimidating air Jacey loathed. "I'm Dr. Mindy Lambert, Jacey's sister."

"She's currently finishing up her residency in El Paso," Jacey put in.

"I'm studying psychiatry," Mindy stated.

"Fortunately, I don't let her practice on me," Jacey said.

Rafferty laughed.

It was, Jacey decided, a beautiful sound.

"I'd advise you to do the same," she continued dryly.

Rafferty nodded, not the least bit intimidated. "So noted." He looked around. "Listen. If you're not done with your visit…"

Mindy held up a hand. "Actually, I've got to get back to El Paso. I was trying to convince Jacey to come home with me, as originally planned. But since she's refused, I'll just have to keep tabs on her and Caitlin another way."

Jacey rolled her eyes. "You really need to work on that overprotectiveness. You should probably see someone."

"Ha-ha." Mindy watched as Jacey settled Caitlin in the Plexiglas nursery bed.

"Seriously, thanks for coming over." Jacey embraced her sister. Despite their differences, they loved each other dearly. "I know how hard it is for you to get away."

Mindy returned the embrace warmly. "I'd do anything for you. You know that." Mindy drew back to look into her eyes. "You call me as often as you can and let me know how you're doing. Promise?"

Jacey nodded, her throat thick with emotion. "Promise," she said huskily.

Mindy bent and kissed her niece goodbye, then headed out. Jacey was so busy watching her sister go, she forgot for a moment they weren't alone.

"So, who's Cash?" a low male voice asked from behind her.

Jacey turned. Rafferty was standing next to the window, one shoulder braced against the glass, his arms folded in front of him. He looked sexy and indomitable. "You heard that?"

"Couldn't help it." Undisguised interest lit his handsome face. "And you didn't answer my question."

Jacey began gathering up the rest of her things. She folded them neatly and put them in her overnight bag. "He's a friend of mine, who donated the sperm for my baby."

Rafferty narrowed his eyes. "You talking literally?"

"It was done in a doctor's office, if that's what you're asking." She could tell by the way Rafferty was looking at her that he was thinking back to the conversation they'd had during her delivery, about the baby's daddy—or lack thereof. "Cash and I agreed from the outset that he would not be responsible for this child." There were, in fact, legal documents verifying this.

Rafferty stepped closer. Arms still folded in front of him, he looked down at the sweetly sleeping Caitlin. "So he's never even going to see this baby?" He looked stunned.

Jacey inhaled. "I'm sure he will at some point."

"But you've got no plans—"

"To call him? I don't even know where he is right now. Last I heard he was headed for the wilds of Alaska to do some dogsledding."

Rafferty regarded her, an increasingly inscrutable expression on his face.

The unexpected intimacy of the conversation left her feeling off kilter. Heart pounding, Jacey picked up her baby and held her close to her chest. "Let me guess. You don't approve." If so, he wasn't the first, and she was sure, he wouldn't be the last.

Ignoring the baby, Rafferty looked her square in the eye. "If you think it's going to be that simple," he concluded gruffly, "you're fooling yourself."

"WHAT'D YOU SAY to tick her off?" Eli asked an hour and a half later.

Rafferty noted his dad's arthritis had eased up, along with the rain. He was moving around a lot more comfortably. But then, that was the way the disease worked. One day his dad would be chipper and spry and ready to saddle up with the rest of them, the next Eli'd be so stiff and sore he'd barely be able to get around. There was just no predicting. Which was why he'd had to retire—and do physical ranch work only sporadically.

However, his dad's intellect, his ability to take in everything around him down to the smallest detail, remained intact.

Bracing himself for a possible lecture, Rafferty rocked back in his desk chair. "What do you mean?"

"I saw the look on Jacey's face when she came in the front door. This should be a very joyous day for her. She was happy when I spoke with her at the hospital yesterday. Now she looks like she wants to punch something. Namely you."

Rafferty went through the day's mail, tossing the junk and stacking the rest. "She told me she had her baby via sperm donor."

Eli sat down. "How in the world did that come up?"

Not easily, Rafferty thought. "I sort of asked her."

"Sort of?"

"Okay, I asked her."

Eli exhaled loudly, his frustration apparent. "Since when are you curious about other people's personal lives?"

Never, Rafferty knew. "I was just making conversation," he fibbed. When, in actuality, he'd had to know the truth. Why, he wasn't sure. It shouldn't matter to him who Caitlin's daddy was, or what that guy might or might not mean to Jacey.

"You need to go apologize," Eli reprimanded.

Rafferty didn't see why. "She didn't have to tell me what she did," he pointed out calmly.

"But she did." Eli thumped the arm of the chair with the flat of his hand. "And as long as she's working here and living in this house—"

"Which is the second bad idea you've had," Rafferty interrupted.

Eli scowled, prompting, "The first being…?"

"Hiring her," Rafferty retorted. He would have had a hard enough time forgetting Jacey Lambert as it was. Now, how the hell was he supposed to pretend she was just the new ranch cook since he had shared one of the most intimate emotional experiences of her life when he'd delivered her baby girl into the world?

"She's an excellent cook. The men love her. We're lucky to have her. As far as where she bunks—" Eli's finger stabbed the air emphatically "—there's no way I'm having a woman and her baby in the bunkhouse. Period. So you need to get used to that."

He was going to have to get used to a lot of things, Rafferty decided. The foremost of which was the way his father was suddenly taking over the domestic front, while still letting Rafferty do whatever he wanted with the cattle business.

His father had a point about one thing. For all their sakes, he did need to steer clear of Ms. Jacey Lambert. Rafferty grunted. "Fine. I'll go tell her I'm sorry I offended her."

And that, he promised himself, was the last thing he would have to do with the dark-haired beauty in quite a while.

Thankful that at least his dad had possessed the good sense to put Jacey and her baby in the opposite wing of bedrooms than the one he and his dad stayed in, Rafferty strode through the ranch house to the bedroom where Jacey would be sleeping.

The door was shut.

Hoping she was already asleep and wouldn't respond, Rafferty rapped lightly.

"Come in. The door's unlocked," she said.

Reluctantly, Rafferty pushed open the door…and practically sunk through the floor at what he saw.

Jacey was seated in a rocking chair, her feet propped up on the footstool in front of her. The zip front of the city-chic pink-and-gray sweats she wore was open. The clinging T-shirt beneath pushed up above her ribs, revealing an expanse of luminous, creamy-soft skin. And although she had a pink baby blanket draped across her shoulder, obscuring all but the baby's feet from view, it was easy to see that Jacey was nursing.

"Sorry." Rafferty told himself to back out of the room— now—but his feet seemed glued to the floor. "Didn't mean to interrupt."

"It's okay." Curious now, she said, "What did you want?"

Seriously? Rafferty thought. You. And that shocked him, too. He hadn't wanted a woman this way in a very long time. If ever.

He swallowed. "I just wanted to apologize if I offended you."

Her smile was soft, contented. Due entirely, he was sure, to the snuggling baby in her arms.

A baby that, previous viewings had confirmed, was every

bit as beautiful and feminine, soft and sweet, as she was. A baby, perversely, he longed to hold. Which again was weird since he had decided two years ago that having a family was just not in the cards for him.

Jacey studied him across the expanse of the bedroom. Bathed in the softness of the lamplight, her hair loose and flowing around her shoulders, she looked incredibly maternal.

She lifted a hand, as cheerful and easygoing as she had been the first night they'd met. "It's okay," she told him with that kind, understanding smile he found so appealing. "You're entitled to your opinion. And I'm entitled to my hormones." Her lips curved ruefully as she admitted with a blush, "I think I'm a little moody. My doc said it will pass as soon as my body adjusts to not being pregnant."

She'd made a lovely pregnant woman, Rafferty thought.

The kind who loved motherhood with every fiber of her being. The kind of woman who should be married and have a dozen kids. Not doing it on her own, with a sperm donor who—to hear her tell it anyway—didn't give a damn.

But again, it was none of his business.

"Hang on a minute." She eased the baby from beneath the blanket. He had a glimpse of the bottom curve of her breast, and then her knit T fell down over her ribs, obscuring all that creamy skin from view.

Immune to the lusty nature of his thoughts, Jacey came toward him, the drowsy Caitlin in her arms. Before he could realize what she was about to do, she had transferred the sleeping baby to his arms, so the infant's face was pressed against his shoulder. "Would you burp her while I wash up?" Jacey asked, as if it was the most natural thing in the world.

Too stunned to resist, Rafferty cradled the incredibly small and lightweight newborn to his chest.

Resisting the urge to bury his face in the downy-soft dark brown hair feathering the top of the infant's head, he called out as Jacey disappeared into the adjacent bath. "I don't know how to…do that…"

It was embarrassing to admit, but he'd never even held a newborn baby before, if one discounted the actual birth three days before. The few kids he'd had the occasion to hold had always been a lot older.

Jacey opened the door a crack and stuck her head out. "Just pat her on the back and walk around a bit."

He heard the sound of water running.

"And be sure you support the back of her neck and head with your hand. She can't hold it up by herself."

Obviously, Rafferty thought.

Trying not to like this too much—he saw now how people got used to it—there was something satisfying about holding a life so delicate and new, so warm and cuddly, in your arms. It made you realize how precious life was. Rafferty frowned as the small eyes closed. "Uh…I think she's going to sleep."

"Keep patting her on the back. She should burp in a minute."

Through the opening in the door, he could see Jacey moving about at the sink, hear the soft sound of soap being rubbed between her hands, on her breasts…? Turning away abruptly, he continued to pace around.

The water was shut off.

"You about done in there?" he said.

"Just need to put some cream on."

Deciding he didn't even want to know what that meant, Rafferty pushed the image of any lotion being applied out of his head and kept walking, back turned away from the bathroom door.

His persistence was rewarded. Caitlin let out a loud burp, more suitable for a carousing college student than a tiny baby.

Laughing, Jacey came out to join them. "Let me just put her down and then I'll be right back," she said.

Her hands brushed his chest as she eased the baby from his arms. Rafferty caught a hint of lavender and baby powder, and then Jacey was gone. He was left standing there, his arms empty, feeling oddly bereft.

IT WAS DISCONCERTING having this big, sexy rancher in her bedroom when she was nursing, but Jacey figured she'd better get used to it since she—and Caitlin—were the only females on Lost Mountain Ranch.

"The bassinet and the rocking chair and footstool are really nice by the way."

Rafferty studied her as if that was hard to believe.

Jacey wondered what he found unacceptable about the nursery items—the fact that they were antiques, or that they were a little on the frilly side, with lacy white overlay linens on the bassinet and pastel needlepoint cushions on the chair and cushion. "The bassinet is even on wheels, with a locking mechanism on the bottom, so I can move it around as I need to." She paused as the next idea hit. "You're not upset that I'm using Evans family heirlooms, are you?"

He gave her the kind of enigmatic look that held her at arm's length once again. "Why would I care about that?" he asked finally.

Wondering if she would ever understand Rafferty Evans and what drove him, she expressed her gratitude. "In any case, it was sweet of your dad to get it out of storage and wash the linens in baby detergent and have it all set up for me."

Rafferty nodded. "He can be very helpful."

As well as annoying in some ways, Jacey guessed. Deciding she and Rafferty may as well be straight with each other, as long as they were going to be residing under the same roof, she continued, "Although…just so you know…I told your father it probably wasn't a good idea to have me here."

He went very still. His expression was as maddeningly in-scrutable as his posture. "So you're leaving the job?"

Jacey couldn't say why, but it hurt her feelings that Rafferty was not as pleased as everyone else to have her on the ranch. Not that he didn't have reason to be irritated with her. She had caused him some trouble. Brought him out in a driving rain. Got her car stuck in a muddy ditch. Gone into labor and forced him—by process of elimination—to deliver a baby on ranch property.

She had also fixed breakfast for the men. And was about to prepare hot meals for them three times a day, through the holidays, as a ranch employee. She would have thought he'd be relieved not to have to worry about feeding the cowboys.

Instead, he kept looking at her as if he'd seen a ghost. And not a particularly nice one at that.

"Would you prefer it if I didn't take the job and left the ranch?" she asked, determined to remain unintimidated by his brusqueness.

He waved her inquiry away with an impatient hand. "It doesn't really matter."

"It matters to me," Jacey countered stubbornly.

Rafferty frowned, his gaze probing her. "Why?" he asked, indifferently.

"Because! I'm trying to figure out who you are—Mr. I Couldn't Remember My Manners If a Snake Jumped Up and Bit Me."

"Snakes don't jump," he said, a muscle flexing in his jaw.

She stepped closer, as if she hadn't noticed how impatient he was becoming. "Or are you 'The Really Nice Guy' who helped deliver my baby? The skill with which you dispense rudeness and inhospitality says it's the first. But the gentleness you exhibited when Caitlin and I needed you, or the way you were holding my baby just now, says that kindness isn't entirely foreign to your nature."

He regarded her with a slow, devastating smile. "I thought your sister was the psychiatrist."

Jacey shrugged. "Her constant analyzing is rubbing off on me."

He came closer, too, daring her with a look. His eyebrow went up. "And what does your analyzing say about me?" he asked softly.

A ribbon of desire swept through her. She had the sense that she was getting too close for comfort, yet could not turn away. "I think you protest too much. That you kind of like the idea of having me here, even if it's only going to be through the holidays." After that, she'd told Eli she would try to find something in her field.

Rafferty rolled his eyes. "Now you are off in la-la land."

"Look," Jacey said, "I may not have trained professionally, if that's what you're worried about, but I am a great cook."

Rafferty blew out a contemptuous breath. "Your skill at the stove has nothing to do with how I feel about this arrangement."

"Then what does?" Jacey demanded, stepping closer still.

"This," he told her gruffly, pulling her into his arms for a steamy, all-bets-off kiss.

It had been way too long since Jacey had been embraced this way. Unable to withdraw from the evocative pressure of his mouth moving over hers, she surrendered to the taste and feel of him. It felt so good to be surrounded by such strength and warmth, to lose herself in a kiss that was so sensual and searing it took her breath away.

She had been kissed before. But never like this, in a way that sent emotions swirling through her at breakneck speed. Never in a way that brought forth such a soul-deep yearning.

Rafferty had figured she'd slap him across the face before their lips ever touched. Instead, logic and feelings had fled. Feelings, need, had taken over. She had wound her arms around his neck and kissed him back passionately. So passionately, in fact, he didn't ever want to let her go. Their lips had just begun to fuse, and already he wanted another kiss that was deeper and hotter and more intimate than the last. And damn her, he thought, as she curved her body into his, if she didn't want it too...

Which was why it had to stop. Now. Before it went any further. He let her go. "Now do you see why it's a bad idea for you to be here?" he asked.

"Maybe for you," she retorted, blushing furiously. "Since you can't control your lust or your tongue."

She swore, realizing too late the way he was taking what she had just said.

"I meant your mouth," she corrected over his chuckling.

His rogue amusement only deepened.

All the more frustrated, she swept her hands through her hair. "I meant your words. Manners. Deeds," she finished flatly.

Rafferty agreed—he shouldn't have kissed her, and she sure as heck shouldn't have kissed him back. But they had and now the passion that had been simmering beneath the surface was out there. Hotter than a fire burning in the grate on Christmas Eve.

"I do have a way of upsetting women."

"That's an understatement and a half."

"That being the case—" he sauntered lazily toward the door "—maybe you should leave."

Chapter Four

"Man, it smells good in here," Stretch said.

"Anything we can do to help?" Curly asked with his lothario smile.

Jacey gave the gravy on the stove another stir, then checked the oven to see that the traditional corn-bread stuffing was almost done. The five hired hands had been hanging around the bunkhouse all morning, taking turns holding Caitlin, and sampling the various Thanksgiving dishes as she prepared them. "You-all can set the table."

"For seven?" Red asked.

Jacey did a quick calculation. Five cowboys, Eli and Rafferty and herself. That made… "Eight."

"You including Rafferty?"

"Yes. Why?" Just because Rafferty had been avoiding her entirely for the last four weeks—she had not seen him once—did not mean he would not grace them with his presence for the ranch's traditional turkey dinner.

"Um…" Hoss hemmed and hawed. "Rafferty doesn't do holidays anymore."

"What do you mean he doesn't do holidays?" Jacey slid the yeast rolls in to bake, alongside the sweet-potato and green-bean casseroles.

Gabby spoke for the group reluctantly. "Well, not since… you know, the thing with Angelica."

"What thing with Angelica?"

Stretch looked uncomfortable. "Fellas, I don't think we should say any more."

Gabby nodded. "It's really none of our business."

"I don't want to get in trouble with the boss," Curly said.

"Me, neither," Red agreed.

"Sorry, Jacey," Hoss said gently. He gave her a look that was equivalent to a pat on the shoulder. "We just didn't want you to be disappointed when the boss didn't show up."

She had passed disappointment weeks ago, when he'd kissed her, and then made sure she didn't so much as lay eyes on him again. Not easy to do, when they were both residing under the same roof, albeit in different wings. "Where is Rafferty?"

"Out working," Curly said.

Red nodded. "He was going to burn the spires off the prickly pear on the south side of the mountain."

"That had to be done today?"

The men shrugged, apparently seeing nothing wrong with it.

IT WAS NEARLY FOUR-THIRTY when the Lost Mountain Ranch pickup his father usually drove bumped along the gravel road that connected the pastures on the property. Wondering what was up, Rafferty put down his propane torch. He shoved the brim of his hat back, waiting. It wasn't long before the driver came into view. Seeing who was behind the wheel, he released a string of swearwords not fit for mixed company. And he was still muttering when Jacey parked in the middle of the lane, left the cab and marched toward him.

She was dressed ridiculously, in a black knee-length skirt that revealed just how much of her baby weight she had already lost, some sort of thin, cream-colored sweater with a lacy collar and a row of fancy buttons up the front, just begging to be undone, and sexy black suede heels definitely not meant for traipsing through the brush.

Noting she didn't look scared or worried, just mad, which meant there was no real emergency, he leaned against a recently sheared prickly pear, crossed one boot-clad foot across the other, folded his arms in front of his chest and simply waited.

When she got close enough for them to converse normally, she demanded, "What is wrong with you?"

"I'm *supposed* to be working in the pasture. *You're* the one who's lost." He hooked his thumb in the direction she'd come. "The kitchen is thataway."

Her soft lips formed an irritated line. "You're a laugh a minute, Rafferty Evans."

He settled in against the cactus. "I think so."

Sparks radiated from her green eyes. "You're also unbearably rude."

Here it came. The lecture he'd heard at least half a dozen times before. Although never from her. He picked up his propane torch, turned around and headed through waist-high brush. "Go away. I've got work to do."

As he half suspected, she stormed after him, giving a little cry when her skirt caught on the spires of a cactus he hadn't yet had time to trim back.

Concerned, he turned around to see her delicately extricating the fabric from the pointed end of the spire. Luckily, she didn't appear to be hurt. "Need some help?"

Another glare. "What I need is for you to talk to me. Why did you skip Thanksgiving dinner this afternoon?"

He let his gaze drift over her lazily. "Shouldn't you be doing dishes or nursing the baby?"

She ignored his rudeness. "The men are doing the dishes for me—they insisted, since the dinner you missed was so fantastically delicious. And Caitlin just nursed and went down for a nap, so they're watching over her, too. They'll call me on the truck radio if I'm needed, which I don't expect to be, since the baby was awake all morning while they fawned over her."

Sounded cozy. "What does any of that have to do with me?" he snapped.

Her eyes moist, she stepped closer. "You hurt your father's feelings."

"I did not."

"Yes," she enunciated plainly. "You did."

Rafferty tensed. "He said that?"

Ignoring the damage it was doing to her shoes and clothes, she waded through waist-high brush. "He didn't have to. I saw his disappointment when you didn't show up and your place at the table went empty."

"First of all—" Rafferty set the torch down once again "—a place for me should never have been set. The men should have told you that."

She tilted her face up. "They did."

He scowled at her. "Then why did you set one?"

Color blushed her cheeks. "Because I figured you wouldn't be that much of a jerk. But then…I didn't know about Angelica."

Once again, Rafferty was caught off guard. Once again, he put his emotions in a box. "No one told you about that. They wouldn't dare."

"Really. Then how do I know her name?"

Good question.

Jacey stepped closer yet. "I get that she broke your heart."

Rafferty's gut twisted. Once again, he found himself defending the indefensible. "My wife didn't get thrown from a horse and lose our baby on purpose."

"You were married?" Jacey interrupted, stunned.

"What's so odd about that? Yes. I was married," Rafferty growled. "And furthermore, I thought you knew all about Angelica." Damn it. She'd been bluffing. And he'd fallen for it.

"I gathered she meant a lot to you, that she was your girl-friend. No one said anything about you actually being married."

"Well. I was." *For better or worse, and mostly, worse.*

Jacey made a face that indicated she was struggling to understand. "And she was *horseback riding* when she was pregnant?" Jacey spoke as if that was the dumbest thing on this earth.

And it had been.

As well as the saddest.

Figuring he might as well answer a few questions—otherwise he'd never hear the end of it—Rafferty said, "She wasn't supposed to be. But Angelica was not the kind of woman who liked to be told no."

"Even when she was carrying your baby?" Jacey said, aghast.

Rafferty shrugged, weary of trying to make sense of the insensible himself. "She thought it'd be okay. She was a natural athlete, an accomplished equestrian, and she'd done it before early in the pregnancy, snuck out to ride, and nothing had happened. So even though the doctor told her not to do it, and I forbid it, she kept saddling up every time no one else was around. And that happened from time to time."

"How did she get thrown?"

"She must have started cramping and bleeding while she was out, and from what we could tell, tried to ride home as quickly as possible to get help. Apparently, during the process, she either fell off or got thrown from her mount. Unfortunately, it was during the fall roundup. It was hours before anyone knew she was missing or figured out where she'd gone…and by the time we did find her, it was too late. Both she and our son were gone," Rafferty recounted miserably. The kindness in Jacey's eyes had him going on, "The only blessing in any of it was that she'd hit her head when she was thrown, and according to the doctors, never suffered in the hours she was unconscious and alone…before her death."

Jacey caught her breath. "I'm sorry."

Rafferty did not want Jacey's sympathy or anyone else's. He'd married for all the wrong reasons, gone ahead and gotten his wife pregnant—as per her wishes, despite his gut instincts to the contrary—and been punished for it.

"So you'll forgive me," he said gruffly, bending to pick up his torch again, "if I'm not in a Thanksgiving or any other holiday mood."

Jacey stopped him, hand to his bicep. "Meaning what?" she asked gently.

Rafferty straightened slowly to his full height. "I. Don't. Do. Holidays," he told her. "Not now. Not ever again."

"That's ridiculous," she chided softly.

Rafferty blinked. "Excuse me?"

"I'm sorry for your loss. I'm really sorry for your loss. But that does not give you license to hurt everyone else around you for the rest of your life. That does not mean you get to hurt the family you have left." Her voice rang with emotion. "Your father might have tried to play it cool on the surface but inwardly he was devastated that you didn't show up for dinner this afternoon. And everyone there saw it, knew it. Except, apparently, you."

Rafferty refused to let her diatribe make him feel guilty. "My dad knows how I feel."

"I'm sure he does." Jacey nodded. "But he has feelings, too. Ever think about that?" Jacey threw up her hands. "No, of course not. You're too busy drowning in grief to notice anything else."

"You're not going to make me celebrate any holidays."

Her brow lifted. "Not even Christmas?"

"Not even Christmas," Rafferty assured bluntly.

"Want to bet?" she challenged.

"As a matter of fact, I do. If I win," Rafferty wagered, "you leave this ranch and never come back."

"Charming. And if I win, you never miss a holiday from this day forward for the rest of your life."

"Deal." They shook on it.

"Now, how about coming back to the house with me?" she asked.

He disengaged his rough palm from the softness of hers. "I'm trying to win my side of the bet, not yours, remember?"

"There's turkey. And stuffing," she taunted.

And a hopelessly optimistic woman serving it. "I'm not eating it," he said flatly.

"Cranberry-strawberry-apple compote."

He shook his head.

Instead of leaving, Jacey followed him around, like a puppy on his heels. A beautiful, sexy, eager-for-love puppy, and he really had to stop thinking like this every time he was around her. Hadn't he gotten involved for lust once before? And been miserable?

"What are you doing anyway?" she asked over his shoulder.

He fired up the torch. "Burning the spires off the prickly pear."

She watched from a distance, fascinated. "Why?"

"Because the cacti underneath is great winter forage for our cattle, but the spires will kill them. They can't digest them, and the spires perforate the intestines."

"Ugh."

"So, once the roundup is complete—usually mid-December—we spend some time burning off the spires in all the pastures."

"Makes sense."

Silence. He went deeper into a strand of thigh-high brush, hoping she wouldn't follow.

And once again was disappointed as she tagged along right behind him. He glanced at his watch. "Seriously. Shouldn't you be tending to the baby or something?"

Unable to step over the dense sage he had just easily stepped over, she went around a thicket of chaparral and guajillo, intending to end up at the same place as he. "Seriously. Shouldn't you be watching at least a little football with the guys?" She looked around, perplexed. "What on earth is that smell?"

IT SMELLED, Jacey thought, like some sort of awful musk.

Animal musk.

And there was a reason, she swiftly discovered as a marauding band of the ugliest-looking wild-pig-like creatures came grunting and squealing out of the brush. She let out a high-pitched scream and stumbled backward. There was no doubt that she would certainly have fallen down, had Rafferty not leaped the distance between them like some superhero and taken her into his arms.

His gallantry was all the encouragement she needed.

She threw her arms around his neck, wrapped her legs around his waist and held on for dear life while he calmly strode away from the grunting pack of menacing animals and headed across the pasture to his truck. Once there, he opened up the passenger-side door and tried to set her down. However, try as she might, Jacey found she could not make herself let go. "Wh-wh-what the hell was that?" She shivered uncontrollably.

"Javelina. They like to travel in bands. Cheer up." He tried, unsuccessfully, to pry her arms from around his neck, then abruptly gave up and let the weight of his chest press against hers, reassuring in a way words could not.

"There could have been as many as forty-five in that group." He looked behind him.

Jacey was relieved they were long gone.

"There were only about ten."

"At thirty pounds each!" And horribly ugly, with grizzled brown-and-black fur, big fat bodies, sharp-looking hooves and skinny ratlike tails. Jacey shuddered just thinking about it. "I don't get why you weren't scared of them." Even now, she couldn't seem to stop shaking or unravel her legs from his waist and her arms from around his neck.

"'Cause they usually don't bother humans, unless humans annoy them first. Then they might charge you and cut and slash you with their teeth. But if you leave 'em alone, then they'll leave you alone."

"So I was in no danger," Jacey concluded in relief.

He cocked his head and gave her a thorough once-over. "Not unless you'd kept screaming."

Abruptly, Jacey realized three things. There was really no reason for him to be holding her like this any longer, if there had ever been. Heat was definitely generating where their bodies connected. And she wanted to kiss him again, way too much for her own good.

"I think you can let me go now," she said quietly, deciding she had made a fool of herself long enough.

His irises darkened seductively. "Or maybe not."

"What?"

He tunneled his hands through her hair. Mischief colored his low tone. "I think I like you just the way you are."

"Indebted to you once again?" She tried to joke her way out of this.

"Grateful," he corrected, mouth lowering to hers, "would be nice…"

Jacey had time to draw one quick breath and then his lips were on hers. She'd thought the first embrace they had shared had been something. It was nothing compared to this. Her heart soared as he angled her head and deepened the kiss, tormenting her with lazy sweeps of his tongue. The next thing she knew, she was kissing him back with an answering passion. Driven by feelings she did not care to identify, she forgot all the reasons why they shouldn't be doing this and allowed herself to sink headlong into the warm seductiveness of his embrace.

Rafferty knew he shouldn't be kissing her like there was no tomorrow, but it had been a hell of a day. Not because he'd felt the grief and guilt he usually felt at holidays since his wife and unborn child had died, but because he didn't feel it.

The loss was still there, but it was muted now. It wasn't part of his everyday life, not the way it had been before Jacey Lambert stumbled into his life.

He couldn't say if it was the way she perpetually challenged and drew him out whenever they were together, or the fact he'd delivered her baby and shared a life-altering experience with her.

Or if it was how he felt when he kissed her. Part conquering hero, part completely besotted fool. All he knew for certain was that he had never tasted lips as sweet as hers, or been kissed back so tenderly. Or wanted a woman as much as he wanted her. To the point that if they didn't end this soon, he would unbutton that sweater of hers, push up her skirt and touch her so intimately it would drive her out of her mind with desire. And if he did that, there would be no turning back. And turning back was what they needed to do.

Rafferty stopped, breathing hard. Calling on every ounce of self-restraint he possessed, he told her coarsely, "I'm not what you need, Jacey."

Even if you are what I want....

"I'll be the judge of that." Hand to his chest, Jacey shoved him out of her way and hopped down from the cab of his pickup truck. She clamped her arms in front of her like a shield. "But you're right," she pronounced. "You do need to find another outlet for your frustration with the hand life dealt you. 'Cause it's not going to be me. We are certainly not getting together this way."

Chapter Five

Jacey had a call from her sister shortly before midnight on Thanksgiving Day. "How was your Thanksgiving?" Mindy asked.

"Good." Jacey shifted Caitlin to her other breast to finish nursing. "Yours?"

"Busy. A lot of people get very depressed this time of year, so the E.R. was full of patients."

"I'm sure you were able to help them."

"I hope so." Mindy sighed, sounding as tired as Jacey felt. "So how is your job search going? Made any progress finding a new position in property management?"

How, Jacey wondered, could she tell her sister that the ranch was really beginning to feel like home…and that she was having second thoughts about leaving?

"None so far," Jacey said honestly. Of course, that was no surprise since she hadn't applied anywhere, or even spent time looking at job postings. "But then, this isn't a great time of year, anyway. Usually, there's not a lot of hiring going on until after the first of the year."

"I've got a lead on a luxury-apartment complex here in El Paso that may be looking for someone in February. I'll e-mail it to you."

"Thanks."

"Have you given any more thought to going to business school? This might be a good time to get an MBA."

Jacey sat Caitlin upright and gently patted her back. Milk bubbles still on her rosebud lips, Caitlin stretched and yawned sleepily. "I don't think I want to go to grad school now." *I'm having too good a time simply being a mom, and cooking for an extremely appreciative audience.*

"What about starting your own business?"

"I'm thinking about a lot of things," Jacey stated carefully. Not wanting to argue with her sister, she changed the subject smoothly. "By the way, I'm going to have to work Christmas."

"Me, too. I was thinking maybe we could get together and have our own holiday on the twenty-seventh of December?"

"Sounds perfect. Caitlin and I will be there with bells on."

They talked a little more, making plans for the holiday.

Caitlin still hadn't burped, so Jacey could not put her down, but she was thirsty. Slipping a soft pink flannel robe over her white jersey pajamas, she walked out to the ranch-house kitchen for a glass of milk.

Phone to her ear, she continued talking quietly to Mindy as she padded through the hall to the atrium. She was nearly to the ranch-house kitchen when Mindy asked, "What about Cash?"

"I don't want to talk about Cash."

"Why not?"

"Because Cash is not relevant." Jacey turned the corner and nearly ran into Rafferty. "Listen, Mindy, I've got to go. I'll call you tomorrow. Yeah, love you, too. Bye."

"What are you doing up?" Rafferty drawled.

She adapted an equally nonchalant posture.

Now, if only she could get her body to stop reacting to his presence. She met his gaze. "I could ask the same of you."

"Been working on payroll and doing the books. You?" Desire, pure and simple, glimmered in his eyes.

"Nursing." She tried without success to forget about the kiss.

He swung open the refrigerator door, peered inside.

While he studied the contents, Jacey studied him. As always, he had showered and shaved after coming in from ranch work. The tantalizing fragrance of aftershave clung to his jaw. He had on worn jeans and an untucked corduroy shirt that brought out the intense blue of his eyes. Thick wool socks. No boots, no belt. Tousled hair. Good thing they had a tiny chaperone.

Determined not to put herself in an emotionally vulnerable position with him, she said, "I gather you ate the Thanksgiving dinner I left for you."

"Was that what it was?"

She feigned immunity to his teasing. "I think you knew that."

He shrugged his broad shoulders. "Food is food. Speaking of which—" he squinted down at the blue ceramic dish in his hand "—this pie looks awfully good. Want some?"

The chocolate-pecan concoction was making her mouth water. "No, thanks. I had a piece earlier."

Clearly trying to push her buttons, he reminded her, "It is a holiday, at least for five more minutes, as you're so hell-bent on reminding me."

"If you must know, I'm trying to lose weight." She would, however, have a glass of skim milk. Caitlin cradled in her arm, she moved past him to the fridge, opened the door with her free hand. To her chagrin, the skim milk was all the way in the back.

"Would you mind just for a second?" She shifted Caitlin from her arms to his.

As she moved food around, he studied the yawning babe in his arms. "Wow, she has grown."

Glad to turn the attention back to her daughter, she said proudly, "She's gained three pounds in the past four weeks."

"Her hair seems lighter. When she was born, it was almost black. Now it's almost blond."

Jacey was surprised Rafferty had remembered that. No one else had mentioned it. But then everyone else had been seeing Caitlin every day, so—to them—the change was more gradual. "Probably gets it from her...father. Although the hair-color thing is typical, from what I understand."

"Speaking of Cash..."

Jacey poured milk. "Not you, too."

"Has he seen his daughter?"

Jacey put the milk bottle back in the fridge. "I think you'd know about it if he had."

He flashed her a contemplative grin. "I'm not with you every second."

"There are no secrets around here," Jacey said.

Rafferty eyed her thoughtfully. "True enough. Is Cash going to see her?"

Jacey leaned against the counter. "I'm sure he will eventually."

Rafferty cuddled Caitlin close to his chest. "But he doesn't have any plans to visit anytime soon?"

Jacey drained her glass and put it in the dishwasher. "I don't know."

"Well, what did he say when you talked to him?" Rafferty persisted.

Jacey flushed. "I haven't spoken to him."

Rafferty's eyebrow rose. "You didn't tell him he had a daughter?"

Jacey eased Caitlin into her own arms. "Cash already knew it was a girl—I found that out at my ultrasound months ago."

Rafferty helped himself to a piece of pie. "Still, you should have called him when the baby was born."

Wishing Rafferty didn't look so damn sexy, Jacey turned her glance away. "I text-messaged and e-mailed him the specifics. He'll get one or the other when he returns to civilization."

"And then he'll show up?" Rafferty put the pie into the microwave to warm.

"If I were still in San Antonio, I'm sure he would drop by— he keeps an apartment in the complex I used to manage. I don't know that he would want to drive all the way out here." Jacey sighed impatiently. "Why are you so intent on making sure that Cash sees Caitlin?"

Rafferty gazed at Jacey with a look that brought to mind long kisses and hotter caresses, then predicted, "Because one look at his baby girl and he's going to fall head over heels in love with her. And that is going to change everything."

BEING CLOSE TO Caitlin certainly seemed to be altering Rafferty. He was all heart every time he was near the infant. Which maybe, Jacey thought, was why he had taken such pains to avoid her and her baby. Because he didn't want to be vulnerable, didn't want to be reminded. She swallowed. "I really am sorry about your wife and child." She hadn't done enough to comfort him on that score.

He shrugged, acceptance shutting out the fleeting sadness in his eyes. "Bad things happen. Nothing you can do about it except go on."

"But have you?"

He set his pie aside without taking a bite. "Now who's treading where they don't belong?" His hands clamped the counter on either side of him.

Jacey settled a drowsy Caitlin in the infant seat she kept in the kitchen and strapped her in. "I'm just saying you should be dating someone."

His jaw tightened. "How do you know I'm not?"

Amazed at how unhappy just the thought of that made her feel, Jacey straightened. "Are you?"

"No." He mocked her with a look. "Are you?"

"No." She tried to disguise her relief that he was single.

"Why not?" he persisted, picking up his plate again.

She watched him savor the sweetness of the pie. "Because I've been pregnant and focused on bringing a baby into this world."

He tilted his head. "I've been grieving."

She could only imagine how hard a loss like his had been. "How long has it been?" she asked softly, wishing they'd talked about this earlier, when he had first told her.

"Two years ago, November first," he reflected.

Jacey did some quick calculations. "So the day I showed up…"

"Was the second anniversary of their death." He put his empty plate in the dishwasher.

That certainly explained his unhappy mood that dark and stormy night. "Guess my timing wasn't the best," she allowed.

He brushed her apology off, letting her know with a look that there were no remaining hard feelings about that. "People kept telling me it would get easier with time," he mused after a moment. "I didn't believe 'em then, but they were right. It does."

"So you're ready to move on." Hope rose within her. She wanted, she realized, to see him happy and living life fully again.

Rafferty exhaled. "I don't know that I could ever go through that kind of loss again…but I think I could enjoy other aspects of a relationship."

"Physical aspects."

He grinned in a way that let her know this was true.

Sexual sparks arced between them.

Refusing to acknowledge how attractive she found him, she shook her head in refusal.

"And the companionship," he added more seriously.

Trying hard not to imagine what it would be like to go to bed with him, Jacey sought out more information on his past. "Were you and your wife happy?"

"She was very beautiful—a city girl, like you."

Which didn't answer the question. Which maybe, Jacey thought, was an answer in and of itself.

JACEY WAS STILL THINKING of Rafferty's romantic past, wondering what else she didn't know about him, when the cowboys headed out the next morning.

Only Eli remained with her and the baby. "You should take the rest of the day off," Rafferty's father advised.

Jacey hesitated. "I'm not sure that's fair."

Eli clamped a paternal hand on her shoulder. "Fall roundup is going to continue for another two weeks. You haven't had any time off since you've been here. You need to be out doing what women do today. Black Friday—isn't that what they call it?"

"Because of all the crowds and holiday sales?"

Eli nodded.

"I'm going to do most of my shopping on the Internet this year," Jacey admitted. "But I would like to get into Summit, look around." She hadn't had time thus far to see much except the hospital, grocery store and pediatrician's office. The weeks on the ranch had left her feeling a little stir-crazy. And she could use some new reading material. She decided to take Eli up on his offer, got Caitlin ready for their outing and left for town.

Jacey's first stop was the library.

Filling out the application form was easy. All she had to do was prove she was a resident of Summit County—and thereby eligible for a card. "I'm working at Lost Mountain Ranch," Jacey explained.

The librarian behind the information desk, a petite and pretty blonde about Jacey's age, smiled. "That's one of our historic ranches," she said cheerfully.

Jacey cradled a sleeping Caitlin to her chest. "How long has it been around?" she asked curiously.

"I'm not really sure. We could look." The librarian typed in another command. "I don't think there are any books written on it, but there are plenty of newspaper articles." She paused. "What would you like to know?"

Whether or not I should stay on there, for starters.

Jacey struggled to contain her emotions. "I'm just trying to learn more about the area in general." *And Rafferty in particular. Was he the kind of man she should even be thinking about getting involved with, never mind kissing?*

Noting Jacey's confusion, the librarian leaned across the desk and confided, "I know this is none of my business, but…watch out for Rafferty Evans. He's left a string of broken hearts from here to Big Bend National Park."

A trickle of unease went down Jacey's spine. "You're saying he's a player?"

The librarian hesitated, then continued typing Jacey's information into the computer, her expression one of quiet distress. "All I can tell you is that I dated him for two months, six years ago. He was so incredibly good to me. I thought we were getting serious. Next thing I know—" she shook her head, remembering "—he's easing away from me, ever so kindly, the same way he eased away from all his other girlfriends when he began to lose interest. Which he always seems to do for one reason or another…. No one thought he would marry at all until Angelica came along. But then," she said, shrugging her slender shoulders dejectedly, "what man in his right mind can resist a beautiful model?"

What man indeed? Jacey thought. "Were they happy?" she asked before she could stop herself.

The librarian gestured unknowingly. "They certainly should have been. They had everything going for them." She paused, her eyes full of sympathy. "I'll say this—it'll be a miracle if Rafferty Evans ever settles down again."

RAFFERTY KNEW something was up. At lunch break on Monday, the hired hands approached him.

"Just out of curiosity, boss," Stretch opened the discussion. "Did you do or say anything to Jacey that might have upset her?"

I kissed her and would have made love to her if we both hadn't come to our senses.

"Yeah, she's been real quiet," Curly said, worriedly.

Red opened his lunch pail. "Happy cooking and taking care of her baby, but otherwise…quiet."

"The thing is," Hoss continued, "we know she's only supposed to be here for a few months, but we don't want her to leave. She's the best cook we've ever had. So if it was one of your moods, or something you said or did—"

"We all know how grumpy you can be this time of year," Gabby put in with a sigh.

It wasn't his fault, Rafferty thought irritably, that he still didn't like the holidays.

"We just want to know what it is," Stretch concluded, "so we can fix it."

Rafferty studied the cowboys.

He hadn't been in the bunkhouse all weekend, and in fact had been taking his usual pains to avoid Jacey.

He had thought—hoped—keeping his distance would please her.

Obviously not.

Rafferty looked each man in the eye. They were all in agreement, all right.

"You really think she might up and leave?" he asked, dread spiraling through him.

A sigh of trepidation echoed through the men.

"We do," Hoss said grimly.

"And we can't let that happen," Gabby insisted.

MIDAFTERNOON, JACEY WAS in Rafferty's study, putting the finishing touches on her updated résumé, when the front door to the ranch house opened and closed. Perplexed—Eli wasn't due back from the Cattleman's Association meeting for another two hours—she looked up.

The purposeful footsteps grew closer.

Rafferty appeared in the doorway.

As always when out working the cattle, he had a fine layer of Texas dust on his clothes and stubble across his handsome jaw. His black hat was drawn low across his brow, his expression unusually somber.

Aware he might not want her sitting in his chair at his desk, she explained, "I couldn't get the printer driver on my laptop to work with your wireless network. Your dad said it would be okay if I used your office equipment."

"That's fine." Rafferty glanced at the baby monitor with a frown. "Where's Caitlin?"

"Sleeping in the nursery." Jacey found herself tensing, too.

"Is everything okay? You usually don't come back to the ranch house in the middle of the day."

He strode closer. "I wanted to check in with you."

She met his gaze. "About?"

He looked over her shoulder, at the information on the screen. "That résumé you're working on."

She leaned back in his chair. "It's tradition, when applying for a job. Funny as it may seem, employers usually want to know your work history and the names and phone numbers of your references."

He countered her sarcasm, "Except here."

Determined not to show any weakness this time, she kept her eyes on his. "I admit this job sort of fell into my lap."

Rafferty walked over to the window. He stood for several moments, staring out at the mountains rising in the distance, before finally turning back to her. "Are you unhappy here?"

"The fellas couldn't be nicer."

He held her eyes for a long time. "Then why are you looking to leave?"

Jacey pulled in a stabilizing breath. "My agreement with your dad was a temporary one. You know that."

Rafferty pressed his lips together ruefully. "The cowboys are hoping you will change your mind, and I know my father feels the same way."

Noting he hadn't said how he felt, Jacey returned, "As much as I hate to admit it, I think my sister has a point. I have nearly ten years' experience in property management. I should continue in that field."

He searched her face. "You enjoy it that much?"

Jacey flushed under his scrutiny. "I like problem solving and helping people live happier, more comfortable lives."

He folded his arms. "You could do that here."

"True." Jacey picked up a pen and turned it end over end. "But I'm already at the top of the career ladder here. There's really no room for advancement."

He edged closer. "If you liked it so much, why did you leave your last job?"

Finding that a lot easier to talk about, Jacey sighed. "My boss had promised me I could set up a small nursery in the property office and bring Caitlin to work with me. Unfortunately, he didn't bother to run this arrangement by the corporate office in Chicago until it was nearly time to process the paperwork for my maternity leave." She sighed. "Suffice it to say, the head office was not happy. There were liability issues involved, and they weren't going to go for it. And the property could not be without an onsite manager, so I had to tender my resignation…and give up my furnished luxury apartment on the premises as well."

"Losing your home must have been tough," Rafferty said sympathetically.

"I had already been planning to go to El Paso to be with my sister Mindy when Caitlin was born—and stay with her during the majority of my maternity leave—so that part of it wasn't such a big deal."

"You seem awfully accepting of the mess," he noted, sitting on the edge of his desk.

Jacey shook her head ruefully. "I'm partially to blame. I should have asked for the agreement in writing much sooner—which would have forced my boss to speak with corporate offices. Had I done that, I would have known, long before I even became pregnant, that it wasn't going to work." She sighed again. "So I'm at fault here, too. And they did give me two months' severance pay, as well as a promise to provide me with excellent references. Almost all of my current salary from this job is going into savings, so when I do leave I'll have a tidy nest egg built up."

Rafferty ran his fingers across the filigreed edge of his massive desk. "Is this something you always wanted to do? Become a property manager?"

She found herself mesmerized by the stroking of his hand. "No. I sort of fell into it in college." She forced herself to look up at his face. "I got a part-time job with one of my previous employer's less fancy apartment complexes, answering phones and showing apartments, and I just got comfortable in that environment really quickly." *The way she had here on the ranch.*

"As you've probably noticed, I'm very adaptable." Too adaptable, her sister Mindy always said. To the point she often forgot about her own wants, needs and desires, in her quest to make other people happy. "Anyway, I worked my way up while I was in school to head manager. From there, I continued to move on to nicer properties, and eventually ended up at the one where I was when I quit. It was great because I always had a furnished apartment with the gig."

"So that stuff in your car?" he prompted.

"Is about a fourth of what I own. The rest of my personal belongings—clothes, books, kitchen stuff—are in storage in San Antonio."

"If we offered you more salary…"

She lifted her palm. "That's not really it." If it were just the amount of money she was making, the time she was able to spend with Caitlin, she would stay. She wouldn't care what it did to her career trajectory.

"More time off?" He upped the ante.

"I've got plenty of time off, between meals." More than she would have at any other job, she knew.

"Then what is it?" Rafferty looked frustrated.

If only he wanted her to stay for personal reasons. But that wasn't the case, and she needed to remember that.

Pushing aside the memory of his kisses and the heat of her response to them, Jacey gave Rafferty the only excuse she felt he would accept. "I'm a city girl at heart." She swallowed and forced herself to hold his direct gaze, even as she fibbed. "I just don't think I would be happy here—" *on this ranch with you, longing for something you are clearly unable to give* "—long term."

Chapter Six

Several hours later, Jacey sat at the head of the bunkhouse table. Caitlin was cradled in her left arm and she had a pen in her right hand. While Eli and the men chowed down on a dinner of jalapeño beef stew and homemade buttermilk biscuits, Jacey said, "You-all know I'm going to be here for Christmas."

Welcoming grins, all around, confirming this was so.

Jacey opened her notepad. "How many of you are going to be here?"

A quick show of hands indicated all.

"So, what says 'Christmas' to you-all?" Jacey asked.

Stretch grinned. "Christmas cookies."

"Don't forget the fudge," Hoss said.

The door opened and Rafferty walked in. The men looked surprised but pleased to see that the ranch scion intended to join them for a meal once again.

Jacey wondered if Rafferty's presence had anything to do with the discussion they'd had in the study earlier. She knew he wasn't pleased at the prospect of having to hunt for another chef. Other than that…she had no clue. Not that it should matter.

Rafferty's father stood and walked over to Jacey. "Why don't you let me hold this little darlin' for a while," he said.

Grateful for the respite, Jacey shifted Caitlin to Eli's waiting arms, then picked up her pen again. "Red, what puts you in the spirit?"

"A Christmas tree," he enthused.

"That's easy enough." Jacey wrote. She paused, shot a glance at Rafferty, and then Eli. "Unless there's some objection…?"

"I think it's a fine idea," Eli said.

Jacey turned her glance back to Rafferty.

"I think we've got room in the budget for it," he said dryly.

Everyone at the table looked relieved. They all knew how Rafferty felt about holidays.

"Gabby, what do you think of when it comes to this time of year?" Jacey asked, determined to make this a Christmas they all would remember.

Gabby shrugged. "Presents, of course."

"Do you guys want to do Secret Santa this year? All put our names in a hat and draw somebody else?" *Except maybe Ebenezer there, at the end of the table.*

"We usually just give gifts to ourselves," Stretch explained.

Hoss winked. "That way we don't have to wrap 'em."

"I do that, too," Jacey admitted with a smile, ignoring Rafferty altogether. "But that's not what Christmas is all about."

There was a long, contemplative silence before Stretch finally ventured, "We could always talk to the Eagle Canyon Children's Home, see what they might need and take some presents over there."

"Now, that's the spirit!" Eli said.

If only, Jacey thought, Rafferty could get it, too.

"You can stop gaping now," Rafferty told Jacey an hour later as they perused the Christmas tree lot in Summit.

"Sorry." Jacey turned to look at him beneath the brilliant

yellow lights. "I just can't get over you volunteering to drive me and the baby into town to pick out a tree."

As they strolled among the rows of beautiful Scotch pines along with other customers, Rafferty slid a hand beneath her elbow. He leaned down to murmur in her ear, "It was either this or help the cowboys with the dinner dishes. This seemed easier."

The light touch, along with his proximity, had her tingling all over. She pivoted on her heel, trying not to inhale the tantalizingly familiar fragrance of his aftershave. She met his glance. "Does this mean I won our bet?"

The corners of his lips turned up. "I'm doing an errand, not celebrating the holiday."

And perhaps, she thought, conjuring up an excuse to spend time alone with her and her baby. Although that was probably just wishful thinking on her part.

"It occurs to me we need to better define our bet."

He rubbed his jaw contemplatively, waiting for her to continue.

"What do you consider actually celebrating Christmas?"

He shrugged aimlessly. "Doing all the things I used to do at Christmas."

Wistfulness swept through her as she thought about what it might have been like to know Rafferty in happier times, before he'd become so aloof and cynical. Yet, at the same time, she empathized with his situation. It wasn't easy, recovering from the loss of a loved one. Recovering from the loss of a child that he'd never had the privilege to know had to be so much harder.

Silence fell and their eyes met. Jacey felt an intimacy she didn't expect welling up between them once again. He looked a little taken aback, too. Maybe because this seemed to happen every time they were alone together.

"Enlighten me, cowboy," she prodded gently, wanting them back on track. "Tell me about Christmases past."

He studied her, as if trying to decide how much he wanted to tell her about what he was feeling. Finally, he released a short breath and said, "I would buy presents for everyone close to me, which isn't as easy as it sounds, since I never know what to get."

"Obviously, you haven't heard. It's the thought that counts."

The deeply cynical look was back in his eyes. "Obviously, *you've* never given anyone the exact wrong thing. It's not a pretty picture. You're better off giving nothing than a gift that ends up insulting them or hurting their feelings in some weird way."

Gift giving could be hard, but it was no excuse not to try at all. Figuring that was a discussion best left for another night, Jacey said, "So back to your traditions…?"

He shifted Caitlin to his arms, to allow her to better inspect the trees. "My mom used to make an incredible gingerbread house. When I was a kid, I helped her."

This was a revelation. She saw him at home on the range, not hands-on in the kitchen. "Were you any good at it?" she asked curiously.

"I think I ate more candy than I put on the house. But…it was fun…and the house smelled incredible when all that gingerbread was baking."

Jacey tried to decide between two elegant pines and found it impossible. She turned back to Rafferty. "What else?"

Affection and memory mingled with the underlying melancholy in his voice. "My mom used to cook two really great dinners for everyone on the ranch. One Christmas Eve, the other Christmas Day. We all went to church. Visited with friends. Wondered what it would be like if we ever actually had snow here. You know, the usual."

Jacey held her breath as she wished he would kiss her again, really kiss her. "That doesn't sound so hard." In fact, it would be simple to recreate.

The problem was, she realized, Rafferty just wasn't interested in making the Christmas of the present anywhere near as satisfying as the Christmases of his past.

"WHAT DID YOU DO this time?" Eli asked half an hour after they had arrived home.

"Care to clarify?" Rafferty inquired.

Eli added another log to the fire. "The two of you just picked out a Christmas tree and brought it back to the bunkhouse, which is something that should have made Jacey extremely happy. Yet she looks more morose than ever. What did you do?"

Hell if he knew what had made Jacey turn hot and cold on him once again. He shrugged. "We were just talking." About Christmas. Which maybe said it all.

"Well, maybe you should stop that," his father advised, replacing the screen. "Seriously, I want that young woman to stay here. So you need to stop doing your best to drive her away."

Rafferty defended himself. "I wasn't doing that!"

"Then what *were* you doing?" Eli probed.

Rafferty threw up his hands. "Being myself."

"Well, maybe you should stop that, too."

Rafferty sighed and changed the subject. He walked over to warm his hands next to the hearth. "I'm having them put the tree up in the bunkhouse."

Eli stood with his back to the fire. "You don't want one in the ranch house?"

Rafferty lifted a shoulder. "Do you?"

Eli wouldn't commit. "Jacey might."

Rafferty swore. His women-reading ability was really rusty. "I hadn't thought of that," he said.

Clearly exasperated, Eli said, "I'll take care of it."

"No," Rafferty interjected quickly. "I'll ask her."

Eli sized him up. "You sure you want to do that?" he asked eventually. "You've already ruined her evening once."

Rafferty winced. "All the more reason I should probably apologize."

JACEY WAS IN THE MIDDLE of nursing Caitlin when the knock sounded on her bedroom door. Figuring it was Eli, she made sure the blanket was draped over her shoulder and across her chest, then said, "Come in."

Rafferty walked in, then stopped in his tracks.

"It's okay," she reassured hastily. He couldn't see anything except the obvious fact she was nursing behind the drape of cloth.

Clearly uncomfortable, he said, "My father pointed out I should have asked you when we were at the Christmas-tree lot if you wanted a tree for the ranch house."

If he'd had a hat in his hand, Jacey noted, he would have been twisting the brim. He didn't, so instead he tucked his hands in the back pockets of his jeans and stood awkwardly, awaiting her reply.

I really have to get out of here before I fall in love with this amazing, confounding, difficult man.

She swallowed. "It's okay. Caitlin and I are going to be leaving on the twenty-seventh for El Paso anyway."

He seemed oddly eager to please. "You could have one in your suite back here. There's plenty of room."

Only one problem with that, Jacey thought. "Can you really see your dad coming in here to enjoy it?"

Rafferty shrugged. "He's got the one in the bunkhouse to appreciate."

Jacey didn't want them going to all that trouble for her. She felt, in some ways, she had disrupted life enough on Lost Mountain Ranch. "I don't think so."

He strode close enough to search her eyes. "You want one, don't you?"

I want you *to want one. I want you to open up your heart again.* But aware that might not be possible, Jacey repeated, "You really don't have to go to any trouble for me, Rafferty."

And that was when Caitlin took it into her own hands to end the exceedingly difficult conversation by grasping the blanket in both tiny fists.

ONE MINUTE RAFFERTY WAS standing in the bedroom with Jacey and Caitlin—although he could only hear not see the baby going to town on Jacey's breast. The next, he was standing there looking at Jacey unveiled.

She was more beautiful than any madonna he had ever seen. Blouse open to the waist, baby pressed to her breast, the other revealed in all its satin-skinned, rosy-tipped glory, she was simply the most incredible woman he had ever seen.

Jacey's mouth flew open in distress, and she let out a gasp.

Knowing the only thing he could give her at that moment was her privacy, he exited the room, shutting the door quietly behind him.

Hours later, he was still aroused. Still wanting her. Wishing he could erase the past so he would be free to love again. So he did the only thing he could do.

He told the men to get started without him the next morning and went into town on some made-up errand instead. Then he stopped by the tree lot run by the civic club and purchased the biggest, most beautiful tree they had, as well as two wreaths and another tree stand.

He drove them back to the ranch, took it all inside, left it where she'd find it and then saddled up and headed out to the range to make up for lost time.

He didn't know what he expected when he got back to the ranch hours later, and showed up for dinner in the bunkhouse for the second night in a row, along with everyone else. But it definitely wasn't what he got. Wreaths on both front doors, a Christmas tree in the living room at the ranch house—in addition to the one in the bunkhouse—and Jacey joking around with the guys, Dad acting as if nothing out of the ordinary had happened.

As if he hadn't gone way out of his way to make sure she had what she needed to celebrate Christmas in a way she'd be happy.

"So what do you fellas want to put on the tree?" she asked cheerfully as they dug into their chicken enchiladas, rice and refried beans.

"I like the electric lights," Gabby put in.

"Especially the colored ones that blink," Stretch said.

"Yeah, I remember we had those one time, years ago," Hoss agreed. "They were real pretty with the glittery ornaments."

Eli turned to Jacey. "We have boxes and boxes of decorations in the storeroom over at the ranch house. My wife collected them. Use whatever you like for both trees."

Before Jacey could even nod her thanks, Eli continued, "Rafferty, would you mind showing Jacey where they are and then carrying out whatever she needs? I've got a meeting tonight."

"No problem," Rafferty said, noting without surprise that Jacey did not look thrilled he'd been tapped for the chore.

Later, she confirmed as much when they were both back at the ranch house alone.

"Just point me in the right direction. I'll take it from there," Jacey said tensely.

"Are you mad at me?" Rafferty led the way to the store-room located behind the garage.

"Why would I be mad at you? You brought me a tree and two wreaths to put up."

Rafferty ignored her polite but aloof regard in an effort to get to the truth. He held open the door, switched on the light and followed her inside. "I figured you would have at least acknowledged it."

Jacey set the baby monitor on top of one of the boxes, then whirled toward him. "Okay. You want to put it all on the table? You didn't have to buy another tree and two wreaths just because you saw my breasts, Rafferty."

"I didn't do it for that reason," he explained, irked she would think he was that crass.

She glared at him, obviously reading something he didn't begin to get into his actions. "Really." She stomped closer, looking as if she wanted to smack him. "Then why did you do it?"

Rafferty shrugged, aware for someone who declared he was not going to celebrate Christmas, his actions did not make any sense. "Because you are right—my dad deserves to celebrate the holiday along with everyone else, as do you, and Caitlin. After all, this is your first Christmas with your new baby and hence worthy of celebrating. So you should have a tree where you live as well as where you work."

She looked him up and down. "What else?" she demanded.

He tried to ignore the pretty color flooding her cheeks. "Under the circumstances, it was the right thing to do."

"Uh-huh."

"Seriously." He came closer, too. "It was."

Jacey tilted her head up to his. "You remember that old saying? You can fool some of the people all the time, and all of the people some of the time, but you can't fool me?"

Rafferty exhaled. Obviously, she was thinking about their embarrassing moment as much as he had been thinking about it today. So they might as well dissect it the way women liked to do whenever anything monumental happened…and get it over with. "Okay, Miss I-Know-A-Hidden-Agenda-When-I-See-It," he said, "I confess," he fibbed. "I did it because I saw your breasts."

"Don't you at least owe me an acknowledgment of your change in attitude toward me?"

He passed on the chance to answer and countered with a question of his own instead. "Don't you owe me an acknowledgment—for the trees and the wreaths?"

"Thank you." Her green eyes glittered impatiently. "And you didn't answer my question."

She wanted to know what had been haunting him? Fine! He let his gaze drift lower, to the soft, womanly swell, before returning, deliberately, to her eyes. "Your breasts are beautiful," he said honestly.

So beautiful, he was hard even now.

Jacey thumped his sternum with the flat of her palm. "Not that kind of acknowledgment, you insensitive cowboy!"

He caught her wrist, held it over his thumping heart. "What other kind is there?"

Her fingers spread across his chest. "You really don't know."

He inhaled the soft, womanly fragrance of her hair and skin. "I can honestly say I haven't a clue."

She wrested her hand free, stepped back a pace. "Well, maybe you'll get one if you keep thinking on it."

"Seriously? That's it?"

She nodded. "Seriously. Now, if you'll excuse me, I need to look for those decorations."

Rafferty had let Angelica and countless women before her be all mystifying and confusing. He wasn't going to let Jacey pull the same old baloney. "Oh, no, you don't." He clamped a hand on her shoulder and spun her around to face him. "You're not going to shut me down without explaining exactly what has you so hot under the collar. If it's the fact that I desire you…" *Now more than ever…*

She looked more aggrieved than ever. "That's it, you don't!"

"Excuse me?" They really were talking different languages.

Resentment colored her low tone. "You've seen the goods. The whole goods. Above the waist. Below the waist. And everything everywhere else. And you've decided you'll pass. This, after kissing me not once but twice like there's no tomorrow!"

Rafferty blinked, so astonished he dropped his hand. "You think I've led you on—sexually?"

Hurt and indignation warred in her gaze. "I don't think you're attracted to me. And why should you be? You were married to a beautiful model!"

"Who, as it turned out, was as empty in here—" Rafferty pointed to his heart "—as a dry well."

Jacey stared at him incredulously. "Yeah, well, she's the only one you married and, unlike me who has stretch marks and the whole just-given-birth thing going on here, she was reputedly gorgeous beyond belief." She released a tremulous breath. "And before that, there was a whole legion of women you dated and discarded for no apparent reason."

Rafferty furrowed his brow. "I don't know who you've been talking to—"

"A woman at the library."

"Ah. Let me guess. One of my ex-girlfriends?"

Bingo! "She said you were a player."

"Who hasn't dated anyone in the last two plus years," Rafferty said, guessing the rest of it.

"Well, no, I didn't know that, but that only means you're pickier than ever about women."

Rafferty could hardly believe they were having their first fight when they hadn't even made love yet. And, he realized suddenly, he did intend to make love to Jacey.

"It means I learned my lesson," he corrected gently, guiding her close once again. "It doesn't matter what a woman looks like on the outside if she doesn't have the goods, as you're so fond of putting it, on the inside. Heart. Soul. Compassion. The ability to get along with and appreciate others. And that's just for starters."

She continued to scowl at him, wanting to believe, yet not quite able to do so. "What else?" she whispered.

"She has to be smart and funny and a little sassy, not to mention unafraid to go toe-to-toe with me, as well as be a damn fine cook. It would probably also help if she knew how to manage a property or two or three."

Jacey blew out an exasperated breath. "Now you're patronizing me."

Like hell he was. He looked into her eyes. "I'm telling you that you turn me on more than any other woman I have ever met." He was being honest. It wasn't helping one iota. Maybe, he thought, because words were cheap. Actions were what she would believe.

Seemingly near tears, she turned away and raised her hands as if to ward him off. "I can't do this," she confessed hoarsely.

Now who was kidding themselves?

"Yes," Rafferty said just as resolutely, "you can."

Chapter Seven

It would have been so easy to turn away…to not let Rafferty kiss her again. Certainly, it would have been the smart action to take. It would have protected her heart, staved off rejection, kept her own deficiencies secret. But when he took her head between his large, capable hands and tilted her face tenderly up to his, all common sense faded. She wanted to feel his lips against hers, wanted to taste the flavor that was uniquely him. She needed to experience lust in its purest, most powerful form.

He felt so good, pressing up against her. This was no drugstore cowboy, or wannabe. Rafferty was the real deal—a virile Texan who knew what he wanted and had no compunction in going after it. And what he wanted right now was her.

"I can't believe this is happening again," she murmured as Rafferty twirled her backward to an old-fashioned reading chaise with threadbare upholstery.

With one arm, he swept away the stack of equally threadbare linens laid on top of it.

The next thing Jacey knew, she was lifted over the mess and set back down, feet firmly on the floor. Her knees were pressed against the back of the chaise, and Rafferty wrapped his arms around her. "I can't believe it's taken so long. Damn,

Jacey," he whispered, kissing her cheek, her ear, her neck, "I want you. I want you so much."

She swallowed. Closed her eyes. Buried her face in the tensile heat of his shoulder. Despite her effort, she wasn't able to contain the conflicting emotions swirling through her. "You say that now…"

"I'll say that for an entirety. Or as you put it—" he grinned wolfishly "—I've already seen the goods."

"And walked away," she remembered, her deepest insecurities taking center stage once again.

His gaze traveled over her face in a frank, sensual manner. Tenderly, he stroked her hair and continued to search her eyes. "Only because I was being chivalrous. If I'd had any inkling you wanted me, too…"

"That's the problem," Jacey informed him bluntly over the tumultuous rhythm of her heartbeat. "Wanting and being able to…" She paused, searching for the right word. "Perform… aren't the same thing."

He brought her closer still, flattening his hand over her spine so they were pressed together. "Yet again…you lost me."

She tilted her face up to his. "I can't…" *even say it!* "I'm not any good at…" She paused, wet her lips. "That is…I've never…actually…" Heavens, this was so embarrassing! Yet, better he know now than find out after the fact.

"Are you saying you're a virgin?" He studied her, perplexed.

"No." Which in her view somehow made it all the worse. She wasn't inexperienced. Just ice cold when she should be white hot. She swallowed around the growing tension in her throat and forced herself to continue. "I'm not. But I might as well be for all my, um, success in the area."

Rafferty sat down on the chaise. He pulled Jacey onto his lap, so she was seated sideways, across his thighs. He kept one arm around her waist. The other lifted her chin. He looked into her eyes, all gentle understanding. "Talk to me. What do you mean you have no success?"

Jacey trembled. She thought she had been embarrassed before. It was nothing compared to how she felt now. "I mean, I can't reach…"

He blinked. "You've never…"

"Climaxed," she informed him miserably, knowing this was part of the reason her previous relationships had dwindled and failed. Her frigidity was too hard on the male ego. Hard on hers as well. Made her not even want to try again, never mind feel so inadequate when she was supercapable in every other way.

"Jacey," he told her softly. "Anyone who can kiss the way you do is definitely able to respond."

Her heart took a little leap at the blatant desire in his gaze. Oh, how she wanted to do what he was urging her to do, and let herself go wild with him. Determined, however, not to repeat her previous mistakes, she caught his wandering hand in both of hers. "I wish it was that simple."

"It is." His lips came down on hers, soft and sure, even as he wrested free of her detaining hold.

"Rafferty…"

Still kissing her, he began to unbutton her blouse, apparently seeing this as a challenge he was more than willing to take on.

"Okay, I admit that feels good, but…" she murmured as he traced the subtle curves, kissing her all the while, gently and seductively, before moving lower still. The next thing she knew, his hand had eased beneath her skirt, slid upward, over the insides of her thighs, until she was arching up off his lap. Moaning her pleasure, she gripped his shoulders, not sure whether she was pushing him away or drawing him near, just knowing she had never felt anything so hot and sensual in her life.

It felt so good to have him touching her that way, so good to be wanted…to let all her inhibitions float away as they kissed endlessly. To feel him gently exploring her there… stroking and loving…until she caught her breath. Maybe it was the postpregnancy hormones…maybe it was all the years of pent-up longing, coupled with intense frustration. All Jacey knew for sure was that she had never felt anything like it, as wave after wave of passion swept through her.

When it finally stopped, she was as weak as a kitten, clinging to him, shocked and dazed. "I know you don't believe in celebrating Christmas anymore, but that was some present," she told him breathlessly, trying to make light out of what had been a very monumental event.

"One question," Rafferty said, kissing her temple as she closed her eyes and rested her forehead against his cheek. He slid a hand beneath her chin and lifted her face up to his. "Just who made you think you couldn't enjoy sex?"

SPYING THE DECORATIONS they had been hunting for all along, Jacey adjusted her clothing and slid off his lap. "It's just something I've always known."

He ambled after her, still looking as if he wanted to make love to her then and there. "Why?"

Doing her best to quell her breathlessness, she stopped and looked into his eyes. "Because I've never been all that comfortable even kissing someone." *Not the way I've been with you….*

He handed her two of the lightest plastic storage boxes and picked up the heaviest two. "Ever stop to think it might have been the fault of the person kissing you?"

"Well, yeah, *now,*" Jacey replied, eager to get out of the

storeroom and away from the possibility of any further intimacy. She practically lost her grip on the containers, her hands were so slick with perspiration. "Because I finally know I *like* what we just…did," she mumbled, embarrassed. A lot! It hadn't felt uncomfortable, hadn't had that underlying ick factor that had always left her feeling more used and invaded than cherished.

He stopped next to the tree in the living room and said softly, "It's more than just my lovemaking skill, Jacey."

Flushing, she set the decorations onto the floor. Leave it to Rafferty to try to build something out of nothing. "I don't know about that. Granted, I've only had two serious relationships."

He opened up a box containing strands of colored electric lights. "Tell me about them."

Jacey untangled a clump of old-fashioned wooden ornaments, in the shape of Nutcracker figurines. "You sure are curious tonight."

He shrugged, not the least bit apologetic. "I want to know everything about you, Jacey."

Their glances held. Realizing the need to know went both ways, Jacey's heart pounded.

"So back to your previous boyfriends," Rafferty prompted.

"Andrew was my college boyfriend. We dated three years, and only started sleeping together at the end. It was embarrassingly awkward and we broke up—he felt he had to sow his wild oats. And I was relieved. I didn't know what lovemaking was supposed to be like, but I was pretty sure it wasn't that.

"The other guy came along about two years later. It took me that long to get up my nerve again, and Patrick wasn't the type to pressure a girl into bed, which I liked. What I didn't like was that it didn't seem to matter to him if we didn't sleep together."

Rafferty quirked an eyebrow but didn't interrupt.

"Anyway, we eventually ended up there and it wasn't a whole lot better than my first experience. But because I had concluded I just wasn't a really physical person—and neither was he—I was okay with it. He thought it was fine, too, and since we got along great in every other aspect of our relationship, we kept dating. Eventually, we started to think about doing something more permanent."

She paused, remembering the shock and the heartache. "And then, one day out of the blue he told me he'd been thinking about it, and he just wasn't sure he ever wanted to be a father. That wasn't going to work for me, so we broke up. Then I just started thinking about how much I really did want to have a child, and I knew if I waited to find the guy to settle down and have a family with that it could be too late. So I started looking into sperm banks."

"And that's when Dash came along," Rafferty guessed, still untangling lights.

Jacey crossed her arms. "His name is Cash. And yes. He heard what I was trying to do from a mutual friend and offered to help. So we went to the doctor's office and one artificial insemination later, it was done."

"That was quick."

"Unusually so." Jacey made no effort to disguise her relief that she'd only had to do that once. "Anyway, I took that as a sign that Caitlin was meant to be conceived exactly that way. And I have no regrets."

Rafferty thought a little. "This Caleb must be some guy."

"Cash," she corrected yet again, pretty sure now Rafferty was mixing up the name on purpose to get under her skin. "And he really is great," she said sincerely.

The doorbell rang.

Jacey looked at him. "You expecting anyone?"

"No. You?"

"At nine at night?" she retorted. "I don't think so."

Rafferty went to the door. Jacey heard him mutter something about another lost tourist. Her sympathy going out to the poor lost soul, she kept right on decorating the tree.

The front door opened on a whoosh of cold night air. Low male voices followed. Familiar male voices. Startled, Jacey nearly dropped her decoration. Still clasping the ornament, she followed the sounds of the decidedly male conversation.

Rafferty gestured expansively at the fit and handsome thirtysomething man who could have come straight out of an outdoor-clothing ad.

The interloper winked at her with affection. "Speak of the devil!"

"Cash!" Jacey cried.

"Hey, sweetheart!" Cash closed the distance between them, engulfed her in the kind of hug old friends gave each other after a long absence. "I was just apologizing to Rafferty here about the late hour. I had a heck of a time finding this place, even with GPS."

Jacey stepped back to survey the golden beard Cash had spent the last few months growing. His hair was shoulder length, the sun-streaked strands clean but unkempt. "What are you doing here?"

He flashed her a wide grin. "Your sister tracked me down. Mindy said I had to come right away, that you were in terrible trouble."

RAFFERTY DIDN'T KNOW whether to be relieved there truly was nothing going on between them—or concerned, given the two had conceived a child together…albeit via medical procedure.

"So what's happening?" Cash asked casually, looking every bit the adventurer in trendy hiking boots and clothing. "I see you had the baby."

"Yes, I did. And she is as healthy as can be."

Cash looked pleased for Jacey, but seemed to have no emotional reaction for himself. "That's great," Cash stated casually. "So what's the emergency? When I stopped by the apartment complex in San Antonio to get my Jeep, I heard you were no longer living or working there, that you'd left rather unexpectedly."

"I was sort of forced out." Jacey explained the situation.

Cash exhaled. "Doesn't surprise me. A lot of rich folks can be pretty demanding. They probably wouldn't like a baby in the office. You know, it would mess with your ability to pay sole attention to them and their needs."

Jacey laughed and shook her head. "You're right. I really should have seen it coming."

"So you're working here now?"

"Temporarily."

Too late, Rafferty wished he and his father had secured a long-term deal for Jacey from the beginning.

At the time, of course, it had suited him as much as it had worked for her. Now he felt differently. He wanted her to stay on.

Cash told Jacey with a friendly protectiveness Rafferty found irritating, "Look, I don't have a lot of money in the bank right now—I spent most of what I earned and what I got from my trust for my adventures the last six months—but I can spot you a couple thousand. Or even let you and your baby move into my place back in San Antonio for as long as you need, 'cause I'm not going to be there much... you know that."

Jacey flushed, clearly unhappy. "We had a formal, written, legal agreement, remember?" she told Cash. "You are not responsible in any way for me or this child."

"I know, but we're still friends, Jacey, and friends help each other out. So if you're in a tough spot, I'm here for you."

As was everyone on the ranch, Rafferty thought, resisting the urge to wrap an arm around Jacey's shoulder and bring her in close to his side.

"Thank you," Jacey smiled at Cash. "But we're doing okay. I'm just sorry that Mindy called you."

Cash chuckled. "She's a pretty traditional gal, huh?"

"She just doesn't get our arrangement."

Neither did Rafferty, truth to tell. How could Cash give away a part of himself, and not look back?

If he had fathered a child with Jacey… Which he hadn't, Rafferty reminded himself. He wouldn't have taken off while she was pregnant. Cash had.

"You want to see the baby?" Jacey asked her friend.

"Sure." Cash grinned.

And, to Rafferty's dismay, off they went.

"What's with all the yawns?" Rafferty asked the cowboys midway through the day.

Stretch opened up the gate of a cattle truck, while Curly and Red guided the half-grown animals up the ramp, for transport to the ranch to which they'd been sold.

"We were all up late last night, raiding the fridge and listening to Jacey's friend Cash tell us stories about some of his adventures."

"He's done some really awesome stuff," Hoss said, checking the numbers on the ear tags of the fully weaned five-hundred-pound calves while Rafferty wrote them down.

"I can see why Jacey likes him," Gabby added, separating out a calf that looked a little on the puny side.

So could Rafferty, unfortunately. The guy was charming, intelligent and authentic, and he clearly cared about Jacey— as a friend.

That rankled. Why, Rafferty couldn't say. He didn't begrudge Jacey her friendships—he admired the devotion she had quickly earned from everyone on the ranch. She was a genuinely great woman, the kind of person everybody liked to have around. He supposed it was Cash's lack of interest in the baby that really stuck in his craw.

Rafferty couldn't understand how a man could father a child, and not be all that interested in his offspring. But it was clear Cash was not.

And on the surface, anyway, Jacey seemed to accept his disinterest.

But could that really be the case?

Would she remain content with the situation as it was, or start to want more out of Cash…if only for Caitlin's sake?

And if so, what would that mean to the man Jacey was involved with?

"Right, boss?"

Rafferty turned to Stretch.

Stretch shut the door on the cattle truck. "Another week or so and fall roundup ought to be over. Right?"

Rafferty nodded. "Good work, guys."

Smiles all around. "Thank you," Hoss said, patting his ample gut, "for finally providing us with a bunkhouse cook who can turn out a meal as totally awesome as she is."

Hoots of agreement followed.

But could they keep her? Rafferty wondered. Especially now that Cash had reappeared on the scene?

He had the rest of the day to brood about it.

By 5:00 p.m., the crew was dog tired and ready to go back and hit the showers and see what Jacey had whipped up in their absence.

They turned their mounts in the direction of the ranch buildings and galloped toward home. Where, as it turned out, after they had taken care of their horses for the night, they had an even bigger surprise waiting.

"LIKE IT?" Jacey's eyes sparkled as the men walked out of the barn. Multicolored outdoor Christmas lights sparkled along the eaves and the porch of the bunkhouse. Evergreen garlands framed the front door. The wreath on the door had been embellished with a big red velvet bow and a half-dozen candy canes. The overall effect, even Rafferty had to admit, was downright festive.

Standing right next to her, looking pleased as could be, was Cash Holcombe. He had a backpack over his shoulder, keys to his truck in hand.

"How'd you get all this done?" Rafferty asked.

Jacey's smile grew wider. "Cash helped me."

Cash, Rafferty recalled, was supposed to take off right after breakfast that morning.

Cash shrugged off the praise. "Least I could do for all the hospitality shown me."

"Aren't you staying for supper?" Red asked.

Cash shook his head. "Already ate. Gotta be on my way." He shook hands with all the men one by one.

His grip was as firm and forthright as he was. "Thanks for giving me a place to bunk last night," he told Rafferty.

"No problem," Rafferty said.

Cash turned back to Jacey. He engulfed her in a big, friendly hug. "I meant what I said, now. You want me to call that friend of mine for you, I will. Her family owns a bunch of apartment complexes in the Austin area. Not as luxe as what we're used to, but they might have an opening for a property manager."

Jacey looked at Cash with a mixture of gratitude and affection. "I'll think about it and let you know."

"Good enough! Fellas." Cash aimed a salute their way. "Happy holidays."

"To you, too, Cash," the men chorused.

The adventurer got in his truck and drove off.

Rafferty felt small for thinking it, but he was relieved to see him go.

"Dinner will be ready as soon as you hit the showers," Jacey told the cowboys.

A collective "yeehaw" was followed by a beeline for the door.

Rafferty remained in the yard with Jacey. He was inexplicably ticked off again, feeling more like Scrooge than ever.

"Well—" she gestured expansively at the decorations "—you didn't say. What do you think?"

"Looks…good," Rafferty admitted reluctantly, wishing he had been the one helping her instead of Caitlin's biological daddy.

They studied each other.

He wasn't sure what she was thinking.

"Where's Caitlin?" he asked finally.

"She's sleeping inside the bunkhouse, in her Pack 'n Play."

More silence, fraught with even more emotion. Rafferty wished he could haul Jacey into his arms and claim her as his, once and for all, so none of this would matter. So he wouldn't have to feel jealous. Or worry about any other man making a play for her, because everyone would know they belonged to each other.

"I would have helped you with that, you know."

"As part of you not celebrating Christmas or any other holiday again?" She dared tease him about things no one else, not even his father, would.

The merry glitter in her eyes had him bantering back. "Part of my demonstrating to you how unaffected I am by all the sights and sounds and routine elements of the yuletide. And any other holiday," he added for good measure.

"Watch out, Easter Bunny."

He liked exchanging quips with her. Almost as much as he enjoyed kissing her and giving her her first-ever climax. "If you need help or anything," Rafferty persisted. *Even in bed.* "Let me know."

She shook her head, her eyes as filled with humor as they were wary. "I sure will, cowboy," she said softly.

ALTHOUGH HE WOULD HAVE LIKED nothing more than to sit across the dinner table from Jacey, taking in her lovely countenance, Rafferty did not go to the bunkhouse for dinner with his dad. He begged off, saying he'd get something later. He wanted to update the books on the computer, accurately record which cattle had been sold to the other ranch.

Eli didn't buy it.

Rafferty didn't care.

He was beginning to get way too involved with Ms. Jacey Lambert and her baby. Before he knew it, he'd not only be feeling like Jacey belonged with him, he'd be thinking Caitlin was his little girl. Both there, like some sort of Christmas gift from heaven above, to take the place of his late wife and the child he had wanted so very much and lost before he could ever enter this world.

And that wasn't so. Jacey was leaving the ranch as soon as

she could arrange for a permanent job and a home back in the city. Caitlin had a daddy. The daddy didn't want her or care about Caitlin. But that didn't change the facts… Jacey was a city girl. A property manager by profession, not a bunkhouse chef. She wasn't interested in marriage. She preferred to go it alone. The ranch couldn't be more remote.

"Rafferty?" a low voice spoke from the doorway of the study.

Jacey stood there, a foil-wrapped dinner plate in her slender hands. She looked pretty as could be, in her dark green suede skirt and matching sweater, with a Santa pin fastened above her left breast. Sad and disappointed, too. She sauntered in, her stacked heels clicking on the wooden floor. "Are you mad at me?"

Mad for you, maybe, he thought, then immediately pushed the inappropriate thought away. He had decided not to go there, hadn't he? Unless something essential changed in their overall situation.

He took his hands off the computer keyboard and rocked back in his chair. "Why would I be mad at you?"

She cleared a place and set the dinner tray on his desk. "For decorating the bunkhouse without running it by you first."

The familiar mixture of womanly perfume and baby powder teased his senses. Again, he played it cool. They were both adults, free to do—or not do—as they pleased. "You don't have to ask. You can do what you want in that regard."

She looked him up and down, before zeroing in on his eyes. "Then why didn't you come over and eat with the rest of us?"

Because I'm falling hard for you. And it's a mistake.

"I had work to do."

She came closer. "So your father said."

Rafferty stood, pushed back his chair. Restless now, he began to pace. "Speaking of work…don't you have some to do?"

She followed him, albeit at a safe distance, just out of reach. "Dishes are all done. I nursed Caitlin and put her down in her crib—she's asleep for the evening."

Which meant, Rafferty thought, she was free. Or as free as a new mommy was likely to be.

She paused, wet her lips. "Your father is in the bunkhouse playing poker with the fellas. They wanted to know if you want to join them."

"Nope."

She scoffed, shook her head. Dark hair spilled across one shoulder, teasing the top of her Santa pin. "That's what they said you'd say, all right."

He wished she would go away before his hard-on got really unmanageable. Insults usually worked. "You're just a fountain of information," he drawled.

Undeterred, she propped her hands on her hips. "And you're just as ornery as can be."

He set his jaw. "I want to be alone."

She glided closer. "First, I want to tell you there is no reason for you to be jealous of Cash."

He snorted. "Is that what you think is going on here?"

She angled her thumb at the center of her chest, announced smugly, "That's what I know is going on."

This wasn't a competition, he reminded himself. He wasn't putting everything on the line for a woman who wasn't planning to stay, who'd never be happy here anyway. He had done that before, to disastrous result. Lost a wife and a child.

"You are really trying my patience, sweetheart," he warned.

"And you are really trying mine," Jacey retorted. She rose on tiptoe, the softness of her breasts pressing against his chest, the wonderful womanly scent of her inundating his senses. "So it wasn't my imagination," she whispered against his lips, her yearning for him as clear as day. "You and I do have a re-markable chemistry, the kind that doesn't fade, even—" her smile broadened "—in the midst of great personal disdain." She moved back as abruptly as she had moved in, put her heels back down on the floor. As the distance between them widened, the welcoming light went out of her eyes. "Don't worry," she said meaningfully, letting him know it had been his loss. "I can show myself out."

Rafferty let her go—as far as the portal. Then instinct took over. She wasn't the only one who wanted. He caught her wrist and reeled her in. "The only thing I want you to show me," he said gruffly, drawing her close, "is this."

Chapter Eight

Hauling her close and ignoring her gasp of surprise, Rafferty lowered his head and delivered a searing kiss. To his satisfaction, Jacey did not pull away, and he let all he had felt during the long tumultuous day come through in another long, thorough kiss. With a quickness that stunned him, she surrendered with a tremulous breath. The softness of her hair and skin, the scent of her tantalizing fragrance waltzed through him and flooded him with desire. His lower body hardened as her tongue swept into his mouth, hot and hungry, and she ran her hands through his hair and brought him closer still.

Her passionate response to him was all the encouragement he needed. With a low groan, Rafferty put the moves on her, too, twining his tongue with hers, drinking in the taste and smell and touch of her, making no effort to disguise how much he wanted and needed her.

He wanted to love her now, tonight, in every way.

She trembled as his hands found her breasts.

He cupped the soft weight in his hands, molding and caressing, and felt her own body tauten in response. He sensed the need pouring out of her, along with the passion.

Unable to help himself, he delivered another kiss, this one

sweeter, more deliberate and provoking than the last. His need to possess her as overwhelming as it was inevitable, he kissed her long and hard, soft and slow.

Until there was no longer any doubt that what they were experiencing was something extraordinary…that she'd made him come back to life in a way he was never alive before.

"Rafferty," she murmured helplessly against his mouth. Wishing. Wanting. Needing. Even as she feared the complications of a physical as well as emotional involvement.

"I want you," he murmured, kissing her collarbone, the side of her neck, the sensitive spot behind her ear.

The surprising thing was she wanted him, too, even if it was only a short-term fling.

The only problem was…

She flattened her hands across his chest and pushed back. Wishing she could, for once, just throw caution to the wind and follow her heart.

"It's too soon after Caitlin," she said shakily.

Abruptly, the light of recognition gleamed in his eyes. "You still can't…"

Briefly, she shut her eyes against the mixture of disappointment and understanding in his eyes. "Not for a couple of days…" She was going to have to see the doctor again, get the official okay.

They exhaled slowly, drew apart.

"It's probably for the best, anyway," she continued, knees trembling, beginning to feel a little panicked at the way she had nearly lost her head. "We shouldn't hurry into anything."

If this was meant to be, they should both be willing to wait for the right time and place, no matter how long it took. If not, well then, that was her answer, too.

"YOUR DAD SAID your mom had a portable sewing machine around here somewhere." Jacey stood in the doorway of Rafferty's study the following evening. "Do you know where it might be?"

Rafferty pushed back from the desk.

Jacey had gone back to her quarters to nurse an impatient Caitlin before dinner was even over this evening. He had missed seeing her. "Storeroom is my guess."

She took a step closer, her green eyes reserved. "Mind if I look?"

"I'll help you." Rafferty stood, noting the faint blush in her cheeks. No doubt she was thinking about what had happened the first time they were in there alone. Or what would have happened last night in this very study if they'd had the all clear from her doctor.

Her chin took on a stubborn tilt. "You don't have to stop what you're doing."

Rafferty wasn't about to let this chance go by. They had precious little time alone, and with his dad off again, this evening for a holiday social engagement... "You kidding? Anything to keep from having to work on the end-of-year inventory information." He fell into step beside her. "So what do you need the sewing machine for?"

She smiled. "I want to make Christmas stockings for the mantel in the bunkhouse."

He hadn't changed his mind about Christmas decorations, but he was sure the cowboys would appreciate it. "You sew a lot?"

She slid her hands in the pockets of her snug-fitting gray flannel trousers. "I did when I was a kid. We didn't have a lot of money for clothes, which made it hard to keep up with fashion trends, so Mindy and I both learned how to sew."

He opened the storage door, turned on the light, stepped inside. "You don't have a sewing machine?"

Jacey paused to look around and get her bearings. "Actually, I do but it's in storage in San Antonio."

Jacey began threading her way through the disorganized jumble of belongings. As she moved past the chaise where they'd had their hot-and-heavy make-out session, he caught a glimpse of round hip and soft breasts. Desire roared through him.

"So what kind of stuff did your mom sew?"

Telling himself to stop thinking about making love to Jacey—that would happen only when she let him know she was ready—Rafferty replied, "Drapes, bedspreads, tablecloths and matching napkins, stuff like that. Never clothes, though."

Jacey paused in the center of the room, frustration turning down the corners of her lips. "Do you know what it looks like?"

Rafferty nodded. "It's in a beige hard-plastic case about the size of a medium suitcase. Has a handle on it."

Jacey threaded her way through excess furniture and stacks of plastic-encased linens that his mother had once rotated on a quarterly basis. "I found a manual typewriter."

And Rafferty discovered something else. Wordlessly, he hunkered down.

JACEY HAD NEVER SEEN that look on Rafferty's face. Reverent, sentimental, emotional.

She put the set of antique Fiesta Ware back in its box and threaded her way through the jumble of stored belongings.

By the time she reached his side, he was sitting on a ripped leather ottoman. He had a stack of picture frames in Bubble Wrap in his hands. He'd already torn the covering off the first.

"You and your parents?" she guessed.

He showed her a color photograph that had to be at least twenty-five years old. "On our vacation to the Sierra Nevadas."

"You all look so happy." Rafferty especially.

Rafferty nodded, admitting this was so. "Every summer the three of us took a vacation. A two-week trip where all we did was hang together as a family."

They looked through the pictures. His mom and dad made a handsome couple—both had such kind eyes, the type of joy everyone wishes for radiating from their faces. As for their only offspring…he was all lighthearted exuberance.

Jacey got to see Rafferty from one to eighteen. "You were a cute kid." Adorable, really. No wonder all the girls around here had been lining up to go out with him.

He winked at her and set the stack of framed photos back in the box. "I'm still cute."

Too cute for her own good, that was for sure. Jacey swallowed to erase the parched feeling in her throat. "When did the vacations stop?"

Regret tautened the lines on either side of his mouth. "When I was eighteen." He reflected pensively. "I thought I was too old to go on trips with my folks—I wanted to vacation with friends. I was too stupid to realize that I could have done both."

"You miss your mom," she said, feeling an intimacy she didn't expect welling up between them.

"Yeah. But I'm thankful. We had so many happy memories. Such good times." He looked at her. "You must miss your folks."

Jacey nodded, allowing, "I do miss my mom, especially at Christmas." She paused, the loss briefly making it difficult to speak. "We always went all out. She had a knack of making everything really special. She taught us both how to celebrate the small things as well as the big. As for my father…I don't really remember my dad. He died when I was just an infant, my sister a toddler. So Mindy doesn't have any memories of him, either."

Rafferty covered her hand with his. "That must be tough."

Jacey sank into his touch, conceding, "There were definitely times when it was. Our college and high-school graduations were particularly poignant. Other times…it's hard to miss what you've never had. The kids I knew who lost their dads at a later age seemed to suffer the loss a lot more than I did."

He searched her face. "Do you ever worry about bringing up Caitlin alone?"

Jacey took a deep breath. "I wonder sometimes if she'll resent me when she's old enough to understand what I did. But my hope is that I'll be such a good mom, I'll give her such a good life on my own, she won't miss having a dad."

He clasped her other hand, too. "And if she does…?"

Aware she hadn't given nearly enough thought to that part of the equation, Jacey shrugged and went back to hunting for the sewing machine. "Then I guess I call Cash and see if he is at least willing to be a friend."

"That's not your only option," Rafferty pointed out. Finally locating the machine under a large plastic sack of unused fabric, he gave her a thumbs-up sign and waved her over.

"I suppose I could ask Santa to bring me a husband slash daddy and put him under the tree with a big red bow."

Rafferty slanted his head at her. "Interesting idea." She watched as he extricated the carrying case and gave her a peek inside. The machine was there, all right. He handed Jacey the sack of spare fabric and the sewing basket, and carried the machine toward the door. "But that's not what I had in mind."

Her heart taking on an accelerated beat, Jacey fell in step

beside him. As the two of them walked companionably through the house, back toward her suite of rooms, she said, "I'm listening."

He paused outside her bedroom door, setting the case on the floor. "The other option is me."

The intent look in his eyes prompted Jacey to go very still. "What are you offering?" she asked hoarsely.

"To be her godfather."

He was serious!

"Caitlin deserves so much more than a disinterested adventurer as the male role model in her life. And until you do marry—"

"I've got no plans to do that." *Unless I fall head over heels in love,* she amended silently.

"—you need someone to watch out for her and love her and be there for every important event in her life. I am volunteering to be that man."

"I CAN'T BELIEVE you're even considering it," Mindy told Jacey over the phone an hour later, after Jacey had relayed Rafferty's offer.

"It makes sense," Jacey insisted. "And I don't have a godfather lined up."

"I'm her godmother," her sister countered. "That's enough."

"For now," Jacey agreed. "But eventually Caitlin is going to want and need a man in her life she can count on to be there during the times she needs a father figure." Just the way they had….

Mindy clucked. "By the time she's old enough for that, you'll probably be married."

Only one man came to mind as a possible groom, and that was ridiculous. By his own admission, Rafferty Evans was not husband material. Lover, rescuer, confidant, yes. A man with a ring in his pocket, no. Jacey pushed the disturbing thoughts away. "What if I'm not?"

Mindy groaned in mock agony. Jacey could almost see her sister dramatically clapping a hand to her forehead. "I knew this was going to happen," Mindy complained.

"What?" Jacey prepared herself for the onslaught of criticism.

"You're getting too comfortable there."

"So?" Jacey could not help the defensive tone in her voice. She knew her older sister was trying to help, but she really wished that Mindy would keep her opinions to herself.

"So…you've got a *daughter to consider,* Jacey. And a career that needs to be focused on, so that you can provide everything that Caitlin is going to require…*especially* if, as you predict, you never marry. I'm begging you…think about what you're doing here…and don't let your momentary needs overshadow the big picture."

Mindy's words stayed with Jacey the rest of the evening. And were still there the following day when she went into town to see the OB-GYN who had taken care of her after Caitlin's birth.

"You're in great shape, all systems go," the doctor said after completing the exam.

Which meant Jacey could make love with Rafferty if she so chose, any time now. The question was, what was she going to do about his offer to be Caitlin's godfather, and how would what she said to *that* affect the rest of their relationship?

"WHERE'S CAITLIN?" Rafferty asked that evening, after Jacey had put the baby to bed in the nursery. As always, he had showered and shaved after he came in from the range that evening. A corduroy shirt was tucked into the waistband of his jeans. The custom boots he wore were made of soft brown leather and buffed to a soft sheen.

Jacey rose and went to the bathroom that connected her room with the baby's. Gesturing for Rafferty to follow, she tiptoed through the bathroom and into the nursery on the other side. Caitlin was sleeping peacefully in her bassinet. They stood, side by side, looking down at her fondly, the tenderness flowing between them almost palpable.

Rafferty really was going to make an excellent father one day, Jacey thought as the two of them quietly exited the room.

"Have you given any more thought to my offer to be her godfather?" Rafferty asked, looking around amiably at the makeshift sewing center she had set up in her bedroom. A folding banquet table from the storeroom served as her work space, while the writing desk beneath the window held his mother's sewing machine.

Jacey pinned the tissue-paper stocking pattern to the holiday-quilt remnant she had picked up at the fabric store in town.

Trying not to think what it would be like to be tied to Rafferty that way, to count on him to protect, love and watch over her child, she said quietly, "I've thought about it a lot, actually."

All afternoon, during dinner with the fellas in the bunkhouse and as she rocked Caitlin to sleep a short while ago.

He rested his hands on the top of a wing chair in the corner. "You're going to turn me down, aren't you?"

He looked disappointed.

She couldn't blame him.

She was disappointed, too.

Aware her heart was racing at his nearness, Jacey picked up a pair of fabric shears and cut around the preprinted shape, being careful to follow the lines. "I appreciate the offer."

"But...?"

"I can't help but think it's one of those promises made in haste that you might someday come to regret. Especially if one of us marries and has other obligations to spouse and children."

He did not appear as if he considered that much of a worry. "What if we don't?"

"You really need to think about this. Make sure that it's not just the need to feel close to someone, if only through the holidays…that's prompting you to do this."

"It's not the holidays. You, of all people, should know that."

"Okay, then your natural gallantry…coming to the fore."

"I'm not *that* nice of a person, Jacey. I wouldn't offer to be godfather to any kid. Caitlin is special—"

"Which is why we shouldn't do anything rash." Jacey set down her sewing shears and looked Rafferty in the eye.

Seeming to realize she was right—this was too much of a commitment, too soon—Rafferty backed off. "All right. I see your point. Just know that my offer stands. If you ever change your mind—or need anything—I'll be around," he promised.

"I appreciate that. It's always good to have backup." And who knew, Jacey thought wistfully, maybe someday…the time and the situation would be right for her to accept such an offer from Rafferty.

Silence filled the room.

Rafferty studied the fabric she'd already cut out. "Nine," he counted, "which means…"

"I'm making stockings for everyone," Jacey said, glad to talk about something else. "Even one for you, seeing as how I'm going to win our bet and all." She chuckled as the flirtatious mood between them deepened. "I'm going to monogram the names on, too. What should yours say? Ebenezer?"

He gave her an amused once-over. "Very funny."

She tingled in every place his eyes had touched, and some places they hadn't. "You're right," she drawled. "Scrooge is much sexier."

Rafferty grinned, obviously reading way too much in what she'd just said. "So you think I'm sexy, do you?"

She held up a hand, ignoring the ornery slant to his mouth. "I know we talked about furthering our—"

He flashed her a satisfied look. "Lessons?"

She sighed in exasperation. "Is that what you call it?"

"Exploration?" he tried again.

"Foolhardiness," she corrected once again.

Disappointment turned his eyes a dark blue. "You're not having second thoughts."

"Actually…I am."

I could fall in love with you, Rafferty Evans. I'm just beginning to realize how much.

"I guess I don't blame you for that. We haven't even been on a date."

She retreated into politeness. "Which would make it even more complicated, don't you think?"

"Nothing wrong with being complicated. Given the fact that we're both intelligent enough to handle complex situations."

And feelings, Jacey thought. Especially the feelings. "True, but I'm also extremely hormonal. Not to mention… sentimental, confused, overly emotional and unemployed in my chosen field."

He flashed her a look that said he would challenge her views in his own way, own time. "So maybe it's time you did something else, lived another place, another way."

"If my sister Mindy could hear you now."

"She'd say?"

"You were a very bad influence."

"Speaking of bad influences." Winking, he took her in his arms.

Her breath caught. "Rafferty."

He lowered his head. "Just one kiss, Jacey. One simple little kiss."

Jacey wanted him, so much, but they couldn't continue, not unless...

"Whoa there, cowboy," she said firmly. "Before this goes any further, we need to talk about how it's going to be—and set some ground rules."

Chapter Nine

Instinct told Rafferty that allowing Jacey to think too much about what was happening between them at this fragile juncture in their relationship would ruin something that was starting to be very, very good. An even bigger mistake would be not allowing her to have her say. "I'm listening."

"First of, all, if this—whatever it is between us—evolves into something more...we both need to know it's not going to ever be more than a fling."

Rafferty did not want to agree to that, but given the way she was looking at him, it didn't make sense to counter. "Okay."

"Second, it's got to be private. No one can know about this."

"Agreed."

She splayed her hands across his chest. "I'm a very private person."

He nodded, serious. "So am I."

"Third..." She paused to moisten her lips. "If whatever happens next turns out not to meet our expectations, there'll be no hard feelings. We'll just forget about it and go on as if nothing ever happened."

Rafferty didn't know how that was going to be possible. He got hard every time he thought about kissing her. And that was *all* the time. Working to keep the triumph out of his voice, he asked, "And what if it exceeds all expectations?"

She relaxed. "Then we'll take it day by day, and enjoy what we can, when we can, without anyone ever finding out we're together until I leave the ranch."

He had hoped she had forgotten about that. Hoped, in fact, she and the baby would stay indefinitely....

"And fourth..." she continued sternly.

Exasperation got the better of him. He flattened one hand against her spine, brought her closer still. "Enough rules."

"But..."

He was afraid if she continued she would talk herself out of it. Threading his other hand through the hair at the nape of her neck, he lowered his lips to hers. "This is the only rule we need."

He cut off whatever she was about to say next with a hot, steamy kiss.

"And what rule would that be?"

"When something feels this good—" *and this right,* he added silently "—you don't question it, Jacey. You just go with it."

And go with it he did. He kissed her until she wanted him and let him know it. Until the bedroom grew hot and close and need took over once again. She drew his tongue even farther into her mouth, and arched against him, pressing her breasts against his chest...burying her hands in his hair.

This may have started as a flirtation, a mutual yearning that had to be satisfied, but over the days and nights that had followed, it had swiftly evolved into something much more important. The truth was, he wanted Jacey the way he had never wanted any woman. And more significantly, he needed her just as desperately.

Sliding his hands beneath her knit top, he swept it off. She flushed shyly and he knew he had his work cut out for him if he wanted her to be as sexually at ease with him as he wanted her to be. Admiring the silky golden glow of her skin, he unfastened the bra and drew it over her shoulders, baring her delicate, maternal beauty to his view.

"Rafferty…"

"Let me look, Jacey. You're beautiful. So beautiful…" His whole body tightened as he caressed the curves of her breasts, her pearling nipples and the shadowy valley in between. Inhaling the sweet scent of her, he slid ever downward. Tasting the silky stretch of skin across her ribs, he dipped his tongue into her navel.

Her whole body straining against him, she gave a little cry as he swept her knit lounge pants and panties down and off, ran his palms across her thighs and gently parted her legs.

The softness of her body giving new life to his, he took her to a pleasure-filled place, until her pulse was beating as rapidly as his.

They moved to the bed.

His clothes were removed as easily as hers.

And then all was lost in the long, steady climb, until he met his goal and her body took up an urgent rhythm all its own. Her pinnacle caught him by surprise, as did her soft cry, the utter lack of restraint. Satisfaction roaring through him, he held her until the aftershocks passed, then moved upward swiftly.

She looked so beautiful in her passion, so ripe and womanly with her cheeks flushed, her lips damp and open. He felt himself responding wildly. He wanted to make her all his, wanted to prolong the pleasure the best way he knew how.

And that was when Jacey took the lead, opened her legs all the more, put her hands on his hips and brought him the rest of the way home, not stopping until he was surrounded by sweet, silky warmth. Lost in the swirling passion, he lifted her hips and went deeper still. Loving her fiercely, stroking her with his hands, kissing her all the while, until she was just as caught up as he. And they were consumed in the swift rise to oblivion and the softer, sweeter aftermath.

Jacey lay on her back, eyes shut. So this was what it felt like to have an orgasm when a man was deep inside you, she thought. What it felt like to be wrapped up in pleasure so thick and all-encompassing it felt as if you were floating in a cocoon of love.

She had never given herself over so completely to anyone, and even as she continued to shudder with aftershocks, she didn't know quite what to make of it.

Was this simply good sex? The kind everyone raved about? The kind of fierce longing and completion that made people lose their heads...and hearts? Or was it something more?

She didn't know. Wasn't sure, at this point, she cared.

All she knew was that it had been so good, Rafferty had made her feel so uninhibited, so complete, so at peace, she wanted to do it all over again. So when he reached for her, kissed his way down her throat and whispered, "Let me love you again, Jacey," she forgot all her rules, forgot the need to be cautious, and simply did.

"CHRISTMASTIME SURE AGREES with you," Stretch said the next morning over breakfast.

"You haven't stopped smiling since you walked in here this morning," Curly added.

"That's 'cause cooking for you fellas makes me happy," Jacey replied, and it was true. That wasn't the reason she couldn't stop smiling, though. And the boss knew it, which was why she hadn't been able to look at him without fear of giving everything away.

Keeping their reckless tryst a secret was going to be a lot harder than she had ever imagined. And not just because she'd never experienced desire anywhere near that satisfying, but because, somehow, her heart had become involved—to a dangerous degree.

If she wasn't careful, she knew she could imagine herself in love with Rafferty Evans.

And that couldn't happen.

The two of them were too dissimilar to ever consider anything more than simply hooking up temporarily. If they were smart, that is.

"You all need to hurry up," Rafferty ordered, gruffer and more impatient than ever. "We got a lot of fence to ride today."

Five minutes later, all the serving platters were scraped clean. The men cleared the table and carried everything to the bunkhouse kitchen. Jacey had their sack lunches ready to go.

A doting Eli reluctantly handed Caitlin back to Jacey. "I wish I could hang out with you all day and hold the baby," he said, "but this is one activity they need my help on."

"We always need you, Dad," Rafferty said, clapping a hand on Eli's shoulder.

"Uh-huh. Seems to me this ranch is running fine without me most of the time."

"If so, it's because I had a great teacher," Rafferty said.

He and his dad exchanged smiles that left Jacey unexpectedly aching for her mother, and the father she never knew. She ducked her head, working to contain her emotion as the men trooped out.

The bunkhouse was extraordinarily quiet.

Too quiet, really.

Quiet to the point of being lonely.

Jacey pressed a kiss to the top of Caitlin's head and settled her into the wind-up swing to watch, while Jacey did the dishes.

The door to the bunkhouse opened.

Rafferty strode back in.

Her heart skipped a beat.

They hadn't had a moment alone since he had left her bed the night before, well before his father got back from town.

"Forget something?" Jacey asked.

Rafferty nodded and kept coming toward her. He took her by the shoulders and tugged her close. "This."

Jacey saw the kiss coming, knew if she was smart she would have avoided it. She wasn't smart where Rafferty was concerned. She was reckless. Foolishly vulnerable and needy—everything she had sworn never to be.

Her previous relationships had been sensible and comfortable. This interaction with Rafferty was anything but practical. It was skyrockets and fireworks and the sweet taste of peppermint melting on her tongue. It was hot, sexy male coupled with a newly awakened woman, and heaven help her, she did not know what to do to get it back under control.

Finally, when her senses were swimming with the taste, touch and feel of him, he lifted his head.

She swallowed. "I thought we were going to keep this quiet." Kissing like this—in the bunkhouse of all places—was reckless as all get-out!

The look he gave her was unapologetic. "Caitlin won't tell."

Jacey aimed a playful punch at the center of his chest. "You know what I mean, cowboy."

He smiled and sifted his fingers through her hair. "They're all out on the ranch, looking for fence in need of repair."

And she was already in way, way over her head. Falling hard for a man who couldn't even bring himself to celebrate Christmas. "Then what are you doing here?" she asked, stepping back slightly.

He caught her wrist before she could make her escape, lifted her hand and kissed the back of her knuckles. "I've got a phone call to make."

The simple touch threw her senses into a riot, made her think of trembling bodies and damp, rumpled sheets. "Is that what you were doing?"

He tugged her closer still. "I will be, as soon as we're done here. And the cowboys were right," he continued tenderly. "You are beautiful this morning, extraordinarily so."

She wondered what it would be like if they had met some other time, some other way. Her breath came even more erratically. "Listen, Rafferty, I know what you're thinking—"

"Do you?"

"—but that's not going to get you back in the sack with me." Not today. Not again, until they both had time to absorb what had happened and make sure this was what they both wanted.

He rubbed his thumb across her lower lip. "I don't want to be back in the sack with you this morning." His voice deepened. "When that happens again, I want to be able to take my time."

She wanted that, too. Struggling to get her emotions under control, Jacey murmured. "Like you did last night."

He leaned down, so his face was next to hers. "Like *we* did last night."

It was all she could do not to throw herself at him again.

His eyes darkened. "Seriously, Jacey, I don't know if I can do this—keep it quiet. 'Cause right now I want to shout it to the world."

"I think we have to," she said. "At least until after the holidays and we see if this is going to be more than a fling."

He shook his head ruefully. "You insist on having one foot out the door."

"Taking this one day at a time is the only way I'm going to be comfortable."

"Okay," he said gently. "I can see I'm rushing you...so I'll pull back."

"Thank you."

"I still want to spend time with you, Jacey."

She wanted that, too. She just didn't think it was wise until she sorted out her feelings. "You know what will happen if we're alone." *What always happened when they were alone.*

He shrugged. "Then bring Caitlin."

Jacey gave Rafferty an admonishing look. "She's proven to be a very poor chaperone. All she does is eat and sleep."

"And smile and cuddle. And make everyone else smile, too."

The tenderness in his tone made her heart melt. "The fellas do love her," Jacey conceded. Every cowboy on the ranch, from Eli down to the youngest hand, seemed to have a soft spot for her daughter.

"We all love her, Jacey," Rafferty reiterated. He looked her in the eye. "Just as we're all fond of you. But that's not what you and I are talking about, and you know it."

Yes, she did. She just didn't know what to do.

"At the very least, you and I should be able to spend time together as friends. Say, on Saturday?"

Jacey bit her lip, aware his persistence was wearing her down. "It would have to be in a way that doesn't draw undue attention."

He leaned forward to kiss her quickly, said confidently, "Leave that to me."

"How come you got all those college catalogs and applications in the mail today?" Stretch asked over dinner that night in the bunkhouse.

There had been an embarrassing array of business-school applications and brochures in the mail that afternoon. "My sister Mindy requested them," Jacey explained.

"You want to go back to college?" Curly said.

No, Jacey thought, suppressing a sigh, she did not.

"Then why does she think you do?" Hoss asked.

Aware Rafferty was looking at her with an even bigger question in his eyes, Jacey replied, "Because Mindy wants me to do more with my life, always has."

"What's wrong with being a ranch cook?" Red huffed.

"Jacey is a property manager by profession," Eli interjected.

Rafferty looked at Jacey, as if it didn't matter to him one way or another. "Do you want to go back to that?" he asked.

She had.

"Yeah, did you like doing that for a living?" Hoss asked.

Aware all eyes were on her, Jacey nodded. "I enjoyed making people happy, and really that's all it is, making sure people's needs are met when it comes to their residences."

"Which is kind of what you do here, too," Curly flashed her his usual grin.

Hoss patted his full belly. "Make us all happy and content."

Everyone nodded approvingly—except for Rafferty, who was busy contemplating what little remained of the beef brisket, potato salad, beans and slaw on his plate. He avoided her eyes the rest of dinner. Eli was a little too quiet, too. It didn't take long to find out why. As soon as she returned to the house and put Caitlin down, Eli asked to speak to Jacey in the living room. Rafferty was there, too.

"Dad has something he wants to talk to you about," Rafferty said.

"Since I'm the one who hired you, I think I should be the one to talk to you about when it is you might be leaving. Or even if you still plan to leave," Eli said. There was no pressure in the older gentleman's tone, just the need to know. Rafferty was equally poker-faced.

And suddenly Jacey knew what she had to do, even though it went against all her instincts. "I agreed to stay temporarily—through the holidays. And I think we should stick to that," she stated firmly, telling herself that no matter what eventually happened between her and Rafferty, terminating her position would definitely be for the best.

Ignoring the searching look in Rafferty's eyes, she swallowed hard and forced herself to go on, as if this were any other business discussion. "You two both know I'm looking for a job in my profession, following up on leads. At this point, I don't have anything solid, but that isn't to say I won't get an interview tomorrow." Especially if she was a little more aggressive in going after the tips she had been given.

She paused. "If you'd like me to help you look for a new cook—or screen applicants—I could do that. I've got experience interviewing and hiring employees at the properties I've managed, and I know the men's likes and dislikes."

She thought but couldn't be sure she saw a brief flash of hurt and disappointment in Rafferty's blue eyes. "We're not trying to push you into leaving," he interjected quietly.

"Certainly not," Eli added quickly. "The fellas all love you, Jacey, and Rafferty and I—we both feel like you're a member of the Lost Mountain Ranch family."

The problem was, Jacey thought, she wanted to be so much more than that.

RAFFERTY WAITED until his father retired for the evening before he searched out Jacey. She was in his study, seated behind his desk, looking intently at the advertisements they had been running for ranch cook. The sight of her so focused brought home the fact that she had a whole other life she was eager to get back to.

Pushing aside the fear that, like his late wife, Jacey was never going to be happy on the ranch long-term, he said, "Thanks for offering to find and screen applicants. We still on for Saturday?"

"Sure. Figure out what we're going to do yet?"

"I'm working on it."

"Good. Listen—" she motioned for him to take a seat on the opposite side "—I think you need to start by running your ad in something other than area newspapers. You're only reaching locals, who probably already have jobs in restaurants, and that's a whole different arena. You need to start placing ads on Web sites that focus on jobs in the food industry. If you would prefer not to pay the fee for that—"

"We'll pay it."

"—you can go to some of the culinary schools around the state, and let them know what you are looking for in a chef. Someone right out of school, looking to further their experience, might jump at the chance to work here."

They were all great ideas, exactly what he would have expected from someone as bright and innovative as Jacey. He would have jumped on them in an instant if he had wanted to replace her.

"What's the problem?" She set down her pen.

Rafferty figured he might as well be honest. "We're never going to find anyone as perfect as you."

She flushed and turned away. "Sure you will."

She didn't look any happier about leaving Lost Mountain Ranch than he was. "I don't think so." He got up quietly and went around to sit on the edge of the desk, facing her. "And the men don't think so, either."

She rocked back in the chair. "It'll be better, Rafferty," she said in a low, strangled voice.

Right now, he wasn't seeing how.

"And there are other considerations besides how messy this could get, if we…"

"Continue our affair?" he guessed.

The flush in her cheeks deepened. "And there is my duty to my daughter." She pushed back the desk chair, stood and began to pace. "I'm going to have to put Caitlin through college one day, and pay for a lot of stuff along the way. I need to place myself in a situation that will offer a lot more potential for advancement."

It was a valid concern. Still, he couldn't help but feel disappointed. He stood, too. "So you are going back to property management."

She pivoted to face him. "Probably, at least in the short run," she confirmed. Silence fell. She met his eyes. "Once I'm back in the city, I'll have more options. I can keep looking for something better." She shrugged and sighed. "Maybe eventually do what I've talked about for years, and open my own business."

This was news. "What kind of business?"

Her lips curved in a self-conscious smile. "Believe it or not, I've always wanted to own a kitchenware and cookbook shop. Kind of like a down-home, Texas version of Williams-Sonoma."

Rafferty smiled back. "I could see you doing that."

Her eyes lit up. "I love to cook. Love cookbooks. Particularly love gadgets that make things in the kitchen a whole lot easier. But—" she went back to pacing restlessly "—that again would take cash to get going, and I don't want to spend my entire savings on something that might or might not work out. Not when I have Caitlin to consider. But enough about that. Back to this ad." She sank down in the chair and picked up her paper and pen, all business once again. "Let's try to craft one together that will attract the kind of employee you need."

No more eager to see her go than before, Rafferty rubbed his jaw. "Let's see. Gorgeous, pregnant, lost…no, that was you."

Her laughter filled the room. "Very funny, cowboy."

Serious now, Rafferty inched closer. With effort, he kept his hands to himself. "It won't be the same around here without you."

Emotion flickered in her eyes, then disappeared. "You'll get over it," she told him calmly.

Rafferty didn't think so. But sensing Jacey did not want to hear that right now, he let it go and went back to the work at hand. He had ten days to get Jacey to see that being a city girl wasn't all it was cracked up to be, ten days to get her to change her mind and convince her to stay on Lost Mountain Ranch. Ten days until Christmas to make his case.

He better get a move-on.

Chapter Ten

"No one has ever sewn me a Christmas stocking before," Hoss told Jacey the following evening.

"They're real pretty," Gabby agreed.

"We ought to hang 'em on the mantel right now," Curly declared.

"Put yours and Caitlin's up there, too," Eli directed with a smile.

Glad the mantel was large and long enough to hold that many stockings, Jacey got them all tacked up, until only one was left. A glance at the embroidered lettering across the tip showed it belonged to Rafferty—who was typically, when the holiday atmosphere heated up—nowhere in sight.

"Where did Rafferty go?" Jacey asked, exasperated she hadn't seen the lonesome rancher slip out in the after-dinner activity.

"He said somethin' about checking on one of the horses down in the barn," Red remarked.

Probably, Jacey thought, so he wouldn't have to ooh and aah over the new decorations. Heaven forbid he actually get all the way into the spirit, along with everyone else. She imagined he figured that it was enough when he occasionally did peripheral stuff, like put lights on a tree. Without actively enjoying himself. "Do you think Rafferty wants his up here or at the house?" Jacey asked Eli matter-of-factly.

Eli shrugged. "You'll have to ask him."

Deciding she wasn't going to let Rafferty backslide from the small but significant progress they'd already made, Jacey decided. "All right. I will. You fellas keep an eye on Caitlin for me?"

"Absolutely." Stretch spoke for the cowboys. "We've all got to have our turn to give her a cuddle before she goes off to the main house for the night, you know."

They weren't kidding about that, Jacey thought. There was no end to the grumbling if everyone didn't get their turn to interact with the bunkhouse baby. Grinning, Jacey grabbed her fitted black suede jacket off the coatrack by the door. "I'll be back as soon as I talk some holiday cheer into you-know-who."

"Good luck with that!" The men were still chuckling when Jacey slipped out the door of the bunkhouse and walked across the yard to the barn. The night was crisp and cold. A full moon shone overhead.

She stepped into the barn. Rafferty was just outside a stall, toward the end. He had what looked like a first-aid kit in his hand. She strode toward him, trying not to notice how good he looked, in a pine-green shirt, dark denim jeans and boots. The set of his clean-shaven jaw gave him a sexy, don't-mess-with-me look that sent another tingle of excitement down her spine.

"What are you doing?" she demanded, stopping a short distance away.

His probing glance made a leisurely tour of her body before returning to her eyes. "Exactly what it looks like—applying liniment and bandages to Rocket's sore leg," he told her.

Guilt washed through Jacey as she realized the beautiful

bay's front right leg did look a little swollen, from ankle to knee joint. "How did he get hurt?"

Hunkering down, Rafferty packed ice around the bandages and secured it with elastic bandage. "He overdid it a little bit today, when we were out chasing down some stray cattle. He's not as young as he used to be."

He straightened and ran a soothing hand down the horse's neck. Rocket leaned into his touch, nickering softly in response.

Rafferty gave him another pat, and a piece of apple, then shut the stall door. He hung the first-aid kit on a hook on the wall and headed for the metal sink.

Jacey watched him lather up. "You're good at this."

He shot her a knowing smile. "Thank you."

"So good I have to wonder why you didn't finish vet school."

He tore off a square of paper towel and dried his palms. He hooked his thumbs in the belt loops on either side of his jeans. "Because one semester in, I knew I didn't want to spend all my time taking care of animals," he said. "I wanted to run a whole ranch. Manage the grasses, make the numbers work, find the right cowboys for the job and make 'em family. So I came back here."

Aware she would be wise not to press him on this, Jacey lounged against the tack-room wall. "Looks like you've done a good job here, too."

He leaned in close and rested a forearm aside of her head. A second later, he was standing directly in front of her. "If I didn't know better, I'd think you were trying to butter me up."

Jacey's throat went dry. "Now, why would I want to do that?"

"I don't know…" He moved away, headed into the aisleway. "Yet."

She hurried to catch up. As she passed the first stall, the

horse inside snorted loudly and pawed the concrete floor. Startled, she jumped back.

Rafferty came to take her arm and lead her past the securely quartered animal. "I take it you haven't spent much time around horses," he said.

Not sure who wouldn't be a little nervous around a thousand-pound animal that stood a good two feet taller than she did, Jacey grimaced. "That would be correct."

"How come?"

"I grew up in the suburbs of San Antonio, remember?" Even if she had wanted to take riding lessons, which she hadn't, there would have been no money for it.

"So I take it you don't know how to ride."

"Also correct."

He stopped in the office, next to the door, at the other end of the stables. He switched on the light and led the way inside. "Ever want to learn?"

"Not sure."

She studied his expression, unable to tell if he was disappointed…or relieved. "Do you think I should?" she asked finally.

His lips took on an implacable slant. "I don't think anyone should do anything they don't want to do." He sat down at the scarred wooden desk and opened up a file with Rocket's name typed across the front.

She watched him update the medical record by hand. "You told me that Angelica was an accomplished horsewoman."

He rocked back in the old wooden swivel chair, folded his hands behind his head. "Riding was the only thing she liked about being here."

Jacey came around to sit on the edge of the desk, next to him. "She knew that going in and married you anyway?"

He turned his gaze away, admitted candidly, "She loved the

ranch at first. Really enjoyed the fact that she had her pick of horses and could ride for miles on such beautiful and challenging terrain."

"How did you meet?" Jacey asked.

Rafferty exhaled. The way he looked at Jacey just then let her know he didn't talk about this to just anyone. "She was doing a photo shoot not too far from here for one of the big fashion magazines," he said, a cynical glint coming into his eyes. "It was a southwestern theme, so they had 'em in evening wear and jewels, out among the cactus. Really ridiculous, if you ask me. But Angelica grew up in Texas, so for her it was like coming home. She thought Summit was a charming little mountain town, and she liked the idea of hooking up with a real cowboy." A shadow crossed his face. "We dated off and on for a couple years. She'd jet in—I'd pick her up—we'd come back here. It was never more than a weekend at a time, for a few months at a time. Maybe if we'd spent more time together...I don't know..." His voice turned gruff as the memories enveloped him. "Anyway, it was toward the end of her career. Thirty is old for her business. She wanted kids. I did, too. So we got married and she got pregnant right away. I thought she'd be as happy as I was about starting a new life. Having a child."

"But she wasn't," Jacey guessed.

Rafferty shook his head. "She was bored out of her mind. She didn't like to cook. She didn't want to decorate. There was nothing—and no one—in town who interested her."

"Sounds pretty miserable," she noted, her heart going out to him.

"For all of us," he conceded. "And I blame myself for that. I talked her into making what we had permanent. I'll never do that again. Try to convince a city girl to stay with me against her better judgment. Because city girls don't belong on a remote ranch like this."

Jacey protested, "I'm a city girl."

"And, after little more than six weeks, already planning to leave."

Not because she felt hemmed in or bored, Jacey amended silently. "Which is why you're so open to a fling," she observed, suddenly not so sure that was a good thing, after all.

His lips compressed. He looked as discontented as she felt. "I'm well aware it might be all we ever have."

"And yet…" Her heart began to race.

He caught her by the waist, pulling her off the desk and onto his lap. "That doesn't mean I'll let the chance to be with you go by unrealized." He lifted the veil of her hair and kissed his way down the exposed column of her throat, to her collarbone.

Unable to help herself, Jacey moaned low in her throat. She splayed her hands across his chest. "This isn't why I came down here."

He threaded his hand through the hair at the nape of her neck, angling her head beneath his, pressed a kiss to the top of her head and her cheek. Yet another on the corner of her lips. "Why did you?"

Her face rested against the incredibly smooth-shaven warmth of his. Had it ever felt so good to simply be held? she wondered. Had she ever felt as safe and protected and wanted as she did when she was in his arms? "Your Christmas stocking." She snuggled against the rock-solid heat of his body. "The fellas and I wanted to know where you wanted that put up—the bunkhouse mantel along with everyone else's, including your father's—or in the ranch house."

He bent his head and kissed her full on the mouth. "Doesn't

matter," he murmured, holding her still as he kissed her even more thoroughly this time.

Forcing herself to ignore the excitement racing along her limbs, Jacey regarded him with mock censure. "It should matter," she said. It should matter a lot. He should want to be as much a part of the Lost Mountain Ranch family gatherings as she did.

His eyes darkening with an emotion she couldn't identify, he released his hold on her. "It doesn't," he stated mildly. "Sorry."

Knees trembling, she slid off his lap and took a deep, bracing breath. "I'm not giving up on winning our bet."

He traced the line of his jaw with the flat of his hand. "Useful information to know," he drawled. "I'm still not going to let you win."

Jacey wished she could kiss some sense into him. "I don't expect you to cry uncle." She mocked his deadpan tone.

"Good." He rocked back in his chair and propped his booted feet on the edge of the desk. "'Cause I'm not going to."

"I've got to get back."

He stayed where he was. When she was halfway out the door, he called after her, "Make sure they all know I'm as ornery and uncooperative as ever."

Jacey rolled her eyes and headed for the bunkhouse.

The fellas were waiting for the verdict.

"Well?" they wanted to know.

Jacey hoped it didn't look as if she had just been kissed. "He said it would be fine if I want to put it on the mantel here."

Mouths dropped open, agape.

"Or the mantel in the ranch house," Jacey quipped as they all began to chuckle. "Or anywhere. He didn't really care."

"That sounds like him," Gabby remarked.

"Yes, I know." Jacey sighed, not sure why she felt so disappointed—given the likelihood of success—but she was. Despite her best efforts... "Rafferty and Ebenezer Scrooge have a lot in common."

"YOU SHOULDN'T TAKE my son's lack of holiday spirit personally," Eli told Jacey as he walked her and Caitlin back to the ranch house. "Rafferty's been this way for years. It started when he was in college, or maybe a little earlier, I can't recall. I just remember every year he got a little less into the spirit of things, and it really used to annoy my wife."

This was news, Jacey thought. She had wrongly assumed it was because he'd lost his wife and unborn baby around the holidays, two years prior. Apparently, his alienation was more deep-seated.

Jacey sheltered her daughter from the brisk December wind. "It didn't bother you?" she asked his dad.

Eli shrugged in the way men did when they didn't want to admit to a particular emotion. "I was just happy to have him around. My wife and I waited such a long time to be blessed with a child, and we only ever had the one... So I figured every moment I had with Rafferty was a moment to count my blessings, and I didn't spend a lot of time worrying about things that in the great scheme of things didn't matter one whit. So Rafferty didn't want to decorate our tree or pick the menu for the holiday dinner. So what? He was here and helped take care of his mom when she was sick. When arthritis forced me to slow down, he stepped up and took over the ranch. And let me tell you, he's done a fine job there, too. He's a good son. And a good man. And one day he'll make someone a fine husband and a fine father."

Jacey chuckled. "If I didn't know better, I would think you were matchmaking."

"Hmm." He held the door for her.

Jacey removed the knit cap from Caitlin's head and set aside the thick blanket that had kept the baby warm on the walk across the yard. "I notice you're not denying it."

Eli's blue eyes twinkled behind his glasses. He looked, at that moment, a lot like Santa Claus. "I'm an old man. Forgive me for wanting everyone around me to be happy."

The backdoor opened and closed. Rafferty walked in.

Eli looked at his son. "As long as you're here," he started in a voice that brooked no argument, "I want to talk to you about the Christmas stockings."

Rafferty looked irritated. He shot her a glare that left her feeling as if she was most definitely *not* on his side. "I already told Jacey she could hang mine wherever she wants."

Hard to believe the two of them had just been kissing a few minutes ago.

"So she told everyone in the bunkhouse."

Rafferty waited, looking more impatient than ever.

"I think we should put something in them," Eli continued.

Now, there's the spirit, Jacey thought.

"Bonus checks," Rafferty suggested.

"In addition to that," Eli specified.

Rafferty's lips took on a cynical slant. "Like what?" he queried. "An orange or some candy?"

"I was thinking along the lines of something more personal that the boys would treasure."

Nice, Jacey thought.

Rafferty looked flummoxed. "Like what?"

"Well, I was hoping you would help me think of what." Eli mocked his son's uncooperative tone.

"I don't know what they'd want," Rafferty grumbled.

Eli beseeched Jacey. "What do you think?"

Jacey shot Rafferty a pointed look, then turned back to Eli. "I think it's a great idea."

"Then maybe *you* should be in charge of doing it." Rafferty stomped off.

Eli and Jacey were left facing each other. "I'll help you figure something out," she promised.

Rafferty stuck his head back in the kitchen. "I think bonus checks would be fine. We can add extra to each one."

Like money solved everything, Jacey thought, knowing it would never replace the personal touch.

"Add extra," Eli said. "We're still getting gifts. And since you won't help, Jacey will assist me." Eli pivoted back to her. "Want to go tomorrow morning?"

"Sure thing," Jacey said, happy to be of assistance to the ranch family that had done so much for her.

Eli smiled. "Nine o'clock fine with you?"

Jacey ignored Rafferty's dark, parting glance. "Nine o'clock is great."

RAFFERTY KNEW the moment his dad got up the next morning he was not feeling well. His arthritis was obviously acting up. He could hardly get around. "Listen, Dad, I'll go with Jacey today."

Breakfast over, Eli moved stiffly back toward the ranch house. Every step seemed to be causing him a great deal of pain. "You will not. This has to be done right."

Rafferty tossed a glance at the cowboys spilling out of the bunkhouse, headed for the barn. "Dad, I'll do it."

Eli shook his head. "We've not done right by Christmas and these cowboys since your mother died and it's wrong. The fellas are family to us and should be made to feel that way! I might not have realized that till Jacey came along, but now I do, and we're not going back to half-baked ways." Eli regarded Rafferty sternly. "I mean it, Rafferty. If you can't do it with the right spirit, it's not going to be done by you."

Rafferty held the door for his father. "I'll do it with the appropriate attitude. I promise. You promise me you'll give those aching joints of yours a rest."

Eli grasped the frame and moved unsteadily through the portal. "I think I might go back to bed."

"The fellas can handle the chores. I'll see that Jacey and Caitlin have a proper escort. We don't want her getting lost to and from the ranch."

Jacey came up behind them, Caitlin bundled in her arms. Clearly, Rafferty thought, she was still upset with him, too. She'd hardly said a word to him all through breakfast.

"I think I can make it to and from town now, Rafferty," she stated irritably.

Figuring time alone together was exactly what he and Jacey needed, Rafferty shrugged off her disclaimer with the same unyielding look she was giving him. "One never knows," he said mildly. "And as Dad just said, this needs to be done by either him or me—as well as you. And it looks like it's going to be me."

"YOU'RE JUST DOING THIS to be alone with me," Jacey accused the moment they hit the road.

Rafferty shot her an amused look. "What man in his right mind would give up a chance to spend the day with a beautiful woman by his side?"

Not Rafferty Evans, it was clear. "Even if the assigned task is Christmas shopping?" she teased.

A satisfied smile curved his lips. "I prefer to concentrate on the perks."

Jacey settled back in her seat and looked out at the peaceful Texas countryside. As long as they were alone, she figured she might as well work on his attitude, even if doing so risked his ire. "Your dad told me you liked Christmas a lot when you were a kid."

He gave her a curious glance. "What else did he tell you?"

Jacey reached for her travel mug of decaf coffee and took a sip. "That your enthusiasm began to wane somewhere around your college years."

Rafferty was silent, his attention focused on the highway.

"Why did you lose interest in the holidays?" Jacey asked softly.

For a moment, she thought he wasn't going to answer. Finally, he shrugged, and adjusted his grip on the steering wheel.

"Somewhere along the line Thanksgiving, Christmas and New Year's became like every other day. The food maybe was a little better, and unless there was some sort of emergency, no one had to work on the ranch. But other than that, it was simply no big deal."

Jacey studied his handsome profile. "And when you were a kid, it was," she guessed.

His forehead creased. "Well, yeah."

"What did you like about the holidays?"

He sent her a quelling glance. "Picking out the tree."

"Which you skipped this year," she pointed out.

"Decorating it," he continued.

"Which you kind of did."

"And music. My mom used to play Christmas music all the time. Sometimes she'd even start listening to it before Thanksgiving." Rafferty grinned as he remembered and shook his head.

Jacey unwrapped a breakfast pastry she had packed and handed him half. "What else did you like about the holidays?"

He accepted the cinnamon roll gratefully. "All the baking my mom used to do. Every day I'd come home from school and there would be a new kind of cookie or candy. Most of which went to friends in the form of holiday dessert platters but there was always plenty for me and Dad to have. And then there was the gingerbread house she would make every year. I believe I mentioned helping my mom with that the first time you grilled me about Christmases past. Any way, those gingerbread houses got pretty elaborate."

Jacey tried to imagine him enjoying Christmas as a young kid. "Sounds nice."

He smiled, recalling. "It was."

"So all that stopped when you were in college," Jacey guessed.

"No. She continued to keep up the traditions. I just wasn't around until the day or so before. I always had to work my part-time jobs off campus, and usually be back around the twenty-sixth or twenty-seventh, so there wasn't a lot of time to join in on the festivities. And, as the years went by, I kind of phased the whole Christmas thing out…"

Jacey considered that. "So really, the fact you're not as into Christmas is as much your fault as anything else."

Rafferty grew silent as they finished their pastries. But she noted he didn't dispute her estimation.

"You want my advice?" Jacey asked finally.

He smirked. "I don't think I'm going to be able to avoid it."

Thinking that if she could get through to him, this could be his best holiday ever, she pressed on. "If you want to get more out of the holiday, try giving more of yourself."

RAFFERTY WOULD HAVE LIKED to disagree with Jacey's assessment, but he knew in his heart it was true. He had stopped participating in holidays when he was working in retail to help pay his expenses while he was in college. To him back then, all December had meant was the pressure of semester exams, combined with long hours, crabby customers and too little pay. There'd been no time to enjoy the kinds of holiday activities he'd had when he was a kid. Instead of lamenting what he was missing out on, he had convinced himself that it wasn't something he had wanted anyway and hence did not matter.

"You're going to enjoy the holidays this year, even if the fellas and I have to tape a smile on your face," Jacey predicted.

Ironically, Rafferty already was. He just hadn't admitted it. But to admit it would be to willingly put an end to their bet, and hence, Jacey's constant attention. And he wasn't ready for that. "I'm not sure you can get that holiday spirit back once you lose it," he fibbed.

"We've got seven more days before Christmas is here." Jacey winked. "And believe me, miracles have happened in less."

Soon after, they arrived in Fort Stockton. They had barely started shopping when Jacey's cell phone went off. Her voice lit up at whatever she was hearing on the other end of the line. "That's great." Her smile broadened. "Yes, that would be fine. Just a minute, please." She put the caller on hold with a push of a button then looked at Rafferty. "Would you mind taking charge of Caitlin for a few minutes? I really need to step outside and take this call while you continue shopping."

"No problem."

She unhooked her BabyBjörn and shifted the wide-awake Caitlin to his waiting arms. Taking her phone, she stepped outside the store. He could see her through the plate-glass windows, talking energetically and smiling.

Caitlin gurgled and grabbed at his shirt with her fingertips.

Rafferty stared down into long-lashed eyes so much like her momma's. "Who is she talking to?" he asked.

Caitlin made a soft cooing sound in reply.

Enjoying the feel of the baby in his arms, Rafferty shifted her a little higher on his chest and patted her gently on the back. He didn't know what it was about this infant. He'd held a few babies over the years, but this child was something special. He felt a bond with her much like, he supposed, he would have felt for his own child…

It was going to be hard to say goodbye to her when Jacey did leave.

If she left…

That hadn't been decided yet.

Jacey came back into the store, beaming. "Good news, I take it?" Rafferty watched while she slid her cell phone into her purse and zipped it shut.

"Pretty good. That was the friend of Cash's family who owns the apartment complexes in Austin. They got my résumé, and they're interested in doing an interview at one of the properties next to the University of Texas." She smiled up at him. "They want me to come to Austin right away, but I told them it was impossible until after Christmas, so we set up an appointment for late on the twenty-sixth. I can drive there from here, and then fly to El Paso to spend a belated holiday with my sister there."

Rafferty struggled to contain his disappointment. This was her life, her decision. "Sounds like you have it all worked out."

Her cheeks took on a happy flush. "I don't have the job yet, but it would be a good one. It comes with a furnished two-bedroom apartment on the first floor of the high-rise, next to the leasing office, and a paid parking place in the underground garage. Full benefits. As well as the ability to have Caitlin with me at all times, since the clientele of that residence is not as demanding as the residents in the luxury adults-only complex I am used to." She took a breath. "The downside is the residents are university students. And with that group, you're going to have a lot more move-ins and move-outs to monitor and process, as well as noise violations and the like."

"I can see where wild parties and babies wouldn't mix."

"It could be a problem. Then again, if—like they said— it's mostly grad students staying there, it may not be a problem at all. I'll be able to tell what the situation is when I go up to scope things out."

"Well, congrats on the interview. I'm happy for you."

"Thank you." Jacey blew out a sigh of relief. "Now, back to our shopping."

Rafferty glanced around the small department store. "I'm not really seeing anything here that I think the fellas would like."

"Me, neither."

They paused, thinking. "Think we might have more luck at a western-wear store?" Jacey reached for the baby.

Rafferty reluctantly handed the infant back over to her mother. Until Caitlin had come along, he had never realized how much comfort there was to be had in simply cuddling a baby in your arms. "Couldn't hurt," he said.

They drove the short distance to the biggest western-wear store in Fort Stockton. Going up and down the aisles, they considered and rejected many an item on the men's side. "There has to be something here for the guys," Jacey said.

This, Rafferty thought, was what he hated about Christmas. Trying to find the perfect gift for someone and finding yourself completely at a loss. "I don't know what," he said, bypassing a display of saddle canteens that weren't as nice as the ones the cowboys already owned.

Jacey paused next to a pair of red cowgirl boots with black

leather scrolling up the sides. She peered inside. "I'd heard about these," she murmured.

"What?" He edged closer, his shoulder pressing hers as he attempted to look inside.

She handed Caitlin to him again. "Western boots with the cushioned sole of an athletic shoe inside."

"You didn't know they made those?"

She wrinkled her nose. "I'm a city girl. The only pair of cowgirl boots I have I got when I was back in high school, to go kicker dancing. They didn't have these then. At least I don't think they did."

"Why don't you try them on."

Jacey looked at the six-hundred-dollar price tag. "A little out of my price range."

"I bet they'd look cute on."

She laughed and put them back on the display. "Stop tempting me. You know I'm not going to have any use for these once I leave the ranch."

True, Rafferty thought.

The real question was, would it be possible to convince her to stay, in the short time they had left?

Chapter Eleven

"How did the Christmas shopping go?" Eli asked that evening when they walked into the ranch house, laden with bags.

Jacey beamed and stowed the unwrapped presents in the broom closet for now. "We found the perfect gift for the guys."

As well as a number of other things for her daughter and friends. The only two people she hadn't yet shopped for were Mindy—because she hadn't yet decided what she wanted to buy her—and Rafferty.

And it would have been hard to do that with the latter standing right beside her. Although she had no idea what would be an appropriate gift for him, either. What did you give a man you'd made love to once?

It wasn't as if they were lovers.

More like friends who had once tumbled into bed.

That was a pretty big difference.

Eli looked at Rafferty.

"We got all the business gifts taken care of," Rafferty stated in the matter-of-fact tone he always used to discuss business transactions. "Jacey was a big help."

Eli nodded affectionately at Jacey. "As she always is." He held out his hands to Caitlin. The baby's eyes lit up as Rafferty handed her over to his father for a cuddle.

"How's your arthritis?" Rafferty asked his dad gently.

Eli pressed a kiss on the top of Caitlin's head, looking as proud as any grandfather. "Better, since I spent most of the day doing heat treatments and resting the joints."

He was moving around a lot easier, Jacey noted happily. Although even when he was visibly hurting, she had never known Eli to turn down a chance to snuggle with the baby, anymore than his son had in recent days.

Knowing everyone must be getting hungry, Jacey told Eli, "About dinner…since I was running so late, we brought a special treat for you and the guys."

Rafferty headed for the door. "If you want to nurse the baby," he said over his shoulder, "I'll go ahead and put the catering trays in the oven to warm."

Thirty minutes later, Jacey entered the bunkhouse.

The cowboys were gathered in the main room, their hair still damp from their after-work showers. "Heard you brought us something special for supper," Stretch said.

"Chinese food." Jacey smiled.

Faces fell.

"I figured it would be a nice change of pace."

The men nodded, less than enthused.

Rafferty looked at Jacey. He'd told her this was a mistake. She'd refused to believe it. "Listen, guys, you're going to love it."

"Hope so," Gabby said.

"I'm starved," Hoss added.

Jacey settled the drowsy Caitlin into her infant swing, facing the table, and brought all the steaming-hot dishes to the table. There were spring rolls with spicy-sweet orange dipping sauce. Crab wontons. Pork dumplings. Entrées included chicken and broccoli, Mandarin beef with spring onions and sweet-and-sour shrimp. Heaping platters of brown and white rice, and two-gallon jugs of orange tea completed the spread. Something, she thought, for everyone.

The cowboys loaded their plates with a little bit of everything.

"Not too bad," Hoss said eventually, "if you discount that Oriental-tasting spice."

Gabby munched on a spring roll. "Odd way to cook vegetables if you ask me, but sort of tasty."

Red grinned. "I think it's pretty good."

"Me, too." Curly concurred.

Jacey looked at Stretch. "It's different," he noted affably at last, "which is probably good, given all the traditional Texas food we're going to be eating tomorrow."

"What's tomorrow?" Jacey asked curiously.

"The Christmas rodeo, put on by the Cattleman's Association."

There went their previous plans to spend some time together, just hanging out, Jacey thought. She could tell by the newly disappointed look in Rafferty's eyes he was just now realizing the same thing.

"We rotate locations," Stretch continued. "This year it's being held at the Martin ranch, about twenty miles from here."

"You're going, aren't you?" Curly asked.

Hoss added, "It'd be a shame for you to have to do all that cooking and then not get to attend."

All that cooking…? Jacey jumped to attention. No one had said anything to her about cooking for a Christmas rodeo.

Eli shot a sharp look at Rafferty. "You did tell her, didn't you?"

Rafferty scrunched his handsome features into an expression of regret. "I, uh, might have forgotten to mention it," he mumbled at last.

A low whistle echoed throughout the bunkhouse.

"Whoa, are you in trouble," Stretch said.

"No kidding," murmured several others.

Suddenly the Chinese food she had brought them for dinner was the least of Jacey's worries. "What am I supposed to cook?" she asked.

"Potato salad," Rafferty said.

"Yeah, we've been bragging about how good it is to all the other hands in the area," Stretch said.

"That doesn't sound too difficult," Jacey said.

"For two hundred," Eli added, with an annoyed look at his son.

"People?" Jacey echoed, stunned.

"Yeah," Hoss added. "And the servings should be on the large side because the cowboys get pretty hungry by evening when the barbecue is served."

Long accustomed to handling whatever challenges life threw her way, Jacey told herself she could do this. "Okay."

"And a dessert," Eli said, glaring at Rafferty as if he was unable to believe how badly his son had messed up.

Now it was getting ridiculously hard. Jacey gulped, working to keep her face expressionless. "Also for two hundred?"

Eli nodded. "But you know what," he soothed quickly, "we'll just go into town tomorrow morning and buy packaged cookies at the supermarket."

Even the cowboys knew that wasn't a good idea.

"Don't be silly," Jacey said, rising to the occasion. This was her job, after all. And when she embarked on something, she never gave it less than her full effort. To do otherwise would be, well, unthinkable. "I can whip up some sheet cakes the same time I'm preparing the potato salad this evening. It'll be fine." Even if she was up half the night and ended up kicking Rafferty in the shins.

"Are you sure?" Eli asked.

"Positive." Jacey stood, knowing she had no time to waste. "That is if you fellas wouldn't mind cleaning up here tonight?"

"No problem," Rafferty said, flushing guiltily.

"Thanks for dinner, Jacey," Gabby added hastily.

"Much appreciated," Eli agreed and the others murmured their assent.

All eyes went from Rafferty to Jacey and back again.

She suppressed her anger with effort.

Curly grinned. "For once in my life, boss, I am really glad I'm not you."

"I THINK I GOT EVERYTHING you asked for," Rafferty said nearly two hours later, walking back into the ranch house with grocery bags in hand.

He knew he had screwed up. And in fact had had plenty of experience doing just that when it came to the fairer sex. He did not yet know if Jacey was going to let him make it up to her.

"Just set it on the counter." Refusing to so much as even look at him, Jacey continued whacking red and white peppermint sticks into decorative bits with a rolling pin.

She already had two delicious-looking chocolate sheet cakes cooling on the counter. Two more in the oven. And, according to her earlier calculations, when she had sent him off with a list of ingredients to purchase before the store closed, half a dozen more to go.

Rafferty came closer.

Damn, but she was beautiful in a temper.

Sensing that was not the thing to tell her, however, he simply said, "I'm sorry."

She snorted. "I'm sure you are *now,* cowboy."

Rafferty moved so she had no choice but to look at him.

"Now who's lost the Christmas spirit?" he teased. Sensing he had struck a nerve, he prodded gently, "Seriously. Why is this such a big deal?"

Her lower lip shot out. "I don't know. Maybe because if this was important to you, you would have remembered. But because it's important to me, it's of little consequence."

It was his turn to be shocked. "Is that what you think?"

A mixture of hurt and resentment clouded her eyes. "It's the way it is."

He grasped her by the shoulders. "It isn't."

She stepped back, away. "If you were supposed to take two hundred head of cattle to a ranch up near Laredo tomorrow morning, would you have forgotten to inform the hired hands who were going to help you?"

Touché. "Probably not."

Her brow lifted. "Not probably," she corrected.

"Okay," he admitted, sufficiently chastised. "Definitely not."

She went back to whacking peppermint into bits. "I rest my case."

"I meant to tell you."

"But…?" she prodded.

He shrugged sheepishly. "With everything we've had going on around here—" *with the way I lose all rational thought whenever I am around you* "—it slipped my mind. It's not too late to let it go…to just go into town first thing tomorrow morning and buy up every bit of potato salad and a whole smattering of desserts."

Jacey's cheeks grew pink. "Is anyone else going to be bringing anything other than homemade food to the Christmas rodeo?"

He caught her hand and kept her close to him, where she belonged. "Probably not."

Once again, she looked as if she wanted to banish him from her life at any second. "Why not?"

"Because," he said calmly, resisting the urge to take her into his arms and kiss her again, "they all have women who can cook on their ranches."

Resentment glittered in her green eyes. "Women who were probably given more advance notice than I got."

Guilt washed through him. "Which is why they would understand if you just did this the easy way."

"I don't want to disappoint the fellas. Or anyone else for that matter."

He understood Jacey took pride in her cooking. And with good reason; she was a fabulous cook.

He also knew she was a new mother. "I don't want you wearing yourself out."

"I'm not your problem."

"You certainly feel like my problem at this moment."

She glared at him.

He took a gentler approach. "So who else hasn't paid homage to your priorities?"

"My two previous boyfriends. My sister, Mindy."

"What about your mother?"

"If anything, she went the complete opposite way, sacrificing way too much of her own life to see that Mindy and I had everything we ever dreamed of. She worked two jobs, sometimes three, to make sure we always had what we needed." She sighed with regret. "She never had the chance to go to college herself—and she really wanted that for us—so she saved every penny she could for us, often going several years without buying so much as a new blouse or pair of shoes for herself."

"You felt guilty?"

Jacey took a bowl of white icing off the counter and carried it over to one of the finished chocolate sheet cakes. "Very. Because we always had what we needed. Although, I did wear a lot of Mindy's hand-me-downs, too."

Rafferty watched as she spread vanilla frosting over the top and sides of the cakes with long, smooth strokes of the spatula.

Jacey sprinkled chips of candy cane over the top of the iced cake. "We had a very small house in a so-so neighborhood, but the schools were good there. Mom did everything she could to make our lives comfortable in ways that mattered—you know, by cooking hot, homemade meals, making sure we did our homework and keeping things neat and clean." She paused, gratitude tempering her low tone. "Our bank account may have been low, but we always felt safe and protected and loved."

Admiring the skill and grace with which she moved about the kitchen, he asked, "Are you going to do anything differently as a mother?"

Jacey took two sheet cakes out of the oven, put two more pans of batter in. "I'm going to try not to ever have to work two jobs. But other than that, I think everything would be pretty much the same." She offered him a spoonful of sweet, delicious icing, took one for herself. "What about you? Are you going to do anything differently when you're a dad?"

Six weeks ago, Rafferty would have said he wasn't going to be a dad. Now…thanks to Jacey and Caitlin's presence in his life, fatherhood seemed in the realm of possibility. He caught her hand and held it. "Next time, I think I would work harder to make sure my wife and child had what they wanted and needed."

Jacey paused, searching his face, even as she leaned into his touch. "So you will marry again?" she whispered.

Rafferty looked into Jacey's eyes. "Yes," he said, aware his heart hadn't felt this full in a long time. "I will."

JACEY WOKE to the sounds of Caitlin stirring. Sunlight was slipping in through the blinds. Stiff and achy from sleeping in one position too long, she rose on her elbows and looked at the clock. Noon! How had that happened? She had only meant to lie down for a few minutes after Caitlin's 8:00 a.m. feeding.

Shoving the hair from her eyes, she rose and headed to the adjoining room. Caitlin was lying in her bassinet, eyes open, looking around. She had worked one arm out of her swaddling blanket and gurgled happily when she saw Jacey.

Her heart filled with love and the kind of contentment she had only dreamed of. Jacey picked her daughter up. Holding her close, she kissed the downy hair on top of her head. "Good morning, pumpkin," she whispered.

Caitlin gurgled as Jacey set her down on the waterproof changing pad. She changed her diaper and then sat down to nurse.

Figuring she was the only one still there—the men had been planning to leave for the Christmas rodeo and barbecue just after dawn to help set up—Jacey donned a cardigan, put her feet into her fuzzy pink slippers and padded out to the ranch-house kitchen.

She'd just fastened Caitlin into her infant seat, when footsteps sounded behind her.

She turned, saw Rafferty stride in. Unlike her, from the looks of him, he had likely been up quite a while. Trying not to think how much she liked the tantalizing scent of his aftershave, she turned her gaze away. "I thought you'd be at the rodeo."

He paused and looked down at her tenderly. "The Martin ranch can be hard to find. I'll drive the two of you over when you are ready to go."

"The food...?" she asked with an easy smile meant to disguise the way she felt.

"We need to have it there by 4:00 p.m., so we've got plenty of time." His glance trailed over her old-fashioned white nightgown with the high collar and placket front, and the unbuttoned pink cardigan she had thrown on. Her hair was a wreck—unbrushed and fashioned into a loose, messy braid that fell over one shoulder.

"I know," she said dryly, holding up a hand. "I look like an escapee from *Little House on the Prairie.*"

He tunneled his fingers through her dark brown hair. "I was going to say you look really pretty this morning. All soft…"

And vulnerable.

"…and pink-cheeked." He tucked a hand beneath her chin and lifted her face to his.

She blushed. "That's one way to put it," she said, warming everywhere his gaze had touched, as well as everywhere it hadn't.

"And here is another way," he murmured, taking her all the way into his arms. He kissed her as if he hadn't been up half the night, too, helping her finish the cooking. Rocking the baby when the baby needed to be rocked. Looking at her as if he wanted to do just this.

Finally, the kiss came to a halt. Rafferty drew back slowly. "As much as I'd like to continue this…first things first." He looked over at Caitlin, who was smiling and cooing, and waving her arms at them. Rafferty chucked Caitlin on the chin, then turned back to Jacey. "Have you had breakfast?"

Jacey smothered a yawn with the back of her hand. "A bowl of cereal and some juice around five-thirty."

He steered her weary frame into a chair at the table. "Then lunch it is."

"You're going to cook for me?"

"I owe you. It's my fault you were up until 2:00 a.m. last

night, finishing the cakes and making the most delicious potato salad I've ever tasted." He opened up the fridge. "Grilled cheese okay with you?"

"Sounds perfect, actually." When she was this tired, all she wanted was comfort food.

He spread four slices of sourdough bread with butter, layered slices of gourmet cheese between them, then slid two sandwiches into a skillet. While that cooked, he quartered Granny Smith apples and brought out a bunch of chilled red grapes.

"Milk for you?"

"Please." Unable to look into his eyes any longer without thinking about kissing him again, she dropped her glance to the width of his shoulders and the hard musculature of his chest. When he turned to plate the sandwiches, her glance drifted lower, to his trim waist and sexy backside. "How many people are going to be at this rodeo?"

"Usually about two hundred." He shot her a glance as he set her meal in front of her. "You'll have fun. There's music and dancing when the sun goes down, around five."

It sounded lively. "What do people usually wear?"

"Denim. Boots. Hats. The men come in jeans, the ladies usually wear skirts, unless they are competing in the rodeo."

Jacey frowned. Since she'd been on call 24-7 at her previous job, as property manager, most of her wardrobe was city-chic business casual. Worse, she'd only brought a small amount of clothing with her—the rest was still in storage in San Antonio. And she still couldn't quite get into the lone pair of prepregnancy jeans she had brought with her.

"I'm going to have to improvise," she murmured at last, sinking her teeth into the buttery, golden-brown crust and melted cheese. "I don't suppose you have a bandanna I could borrow…?"

RAFFERTY KNEW WOMEN could be particular about their appearance, but this was getting ridiculous.

Cradling Caitlin—who was dressed to the nines herself in a red velvet infant outfit and matching cap—to his chest, he knocked on Jacey's bedroom door. "You about ready in there?"

"Hold your horses, I'm coming!"

Jacey swung open the door.

She looked so incredible she took his breath away.

Her body was draped in a black skirt that barely hit her knees, and a red silk blouse, worn open at the neck, clung to her curves. A red-and-black bandanna was knotted around her neck, the ties to one side. Black tights, black suede stack-heeled loafers—which were still a little worse for the wear after her trek through the canyon earlier in the month—and a black suede jacket completed her outfit. "It's the best I can do."

Her best was pretty damn good.

He'd thought she looked incredible just tumbling out of bed, in that ridiculously frilly nightgown and cardigan. She looked gorgeous now in the sophisticated, city-girl way that he was fast coming to love.

"My hat and boots are in storage in San Antonio."

Rafferty thought back to the pair of six-hundred-dollar boots she had admired at the western-wear store. He should have bought them for her then. She deserved that and so much more.

"I gather you haven't worn them in a while?" he asked casually.

Jacey's eyes filled with remorse. "Several years actually, which is a shame, because I really like kicker dancing." After slinging a diaper bag and purse over her arm, she accompanied Rafferty out to the kitchen, where the food was boxed up and waiting. "How long does this party last?"

Rafferty shifted the baby to her. "They'll have fireworks

at midnight, and everyone will probably disband some time after that."

Jacey hesitated. "Then I should drive, too, because I'm going to want to come home early."

"I'll take you both ways." He pressed a finger against her lips, cutting off the protest he knew was coming. "I don't want you and Caitlin getting lost again on mountain roads, late at night."

She searched his eyes. "You're sure you don't mind?"

Rafferty wrapped a protective arm around her shoulders, and being careful not to crowd the baby in her arms, leaned over to kiss her tenderly. "It's my privilege."

THIS WASN'T A DATE, Jacey told herself firmly as they walked into the Christmas rodeo. But it felt like a date.

Starting with the way everyone looked at them, and the way Rafferty never left her and Caitlin's side. He held the baby as much as she did. Introduced them both around to the ranchers and their families and the hired help that ran those spreads.

Jacey felt welcome in a soul-deep way she never had before. So much so that by the time the band warmed up and the music started she was beginning to wonder if her growing relationship with Rafferty was such a good thing.

"Something on your mind?" Rafferty asked when he finally led her onto the dance floor that had been erected over the lawn.

Jacey looked over at Caitlin, who was happily ensconced in Eli's arms. "I was thinking how good your father is with my baby girl," she fibbed.

He gathered her into his arms. "Besides that."

I was thinking I might be getting too close to you.

Wary of giving too much of her feelings away, Jacey concentrated on following his lead as they two-stepped to the lively beat. "I was thinking how happy everyone is to see you here tonight, with your party attitude on."

It was such a change from the way he had been when she had accidentally trespassed on his ranch nearly seven weeks before.

"Been a while," he admitted, twirling her around.

Their midriffs touched as she went back into his arms. "Any particular reason why?"

One hand clasping hers, the other anchored at her waist, he gazed down at her and said very softly, "I think you know the answer to that."

She wanted to believe it was her.

Trying not to think how much she was enjoying dancing with him—almost as much as she enjoyed making love with him—Jacey cleared her throat. "So…have you decided what you want for Christmas this year?"

"This your way of trying to win our bet? By coaxing me into revealing a gift list?"

She needed to gift him with something, if only as a thank-you for giving her a place to stay, rising to an emergency situation and delivering Caitlin into the world. "You must want something," she insisted, knowing she wanted to win so much more than a simple bet with him—she wanted to win his *heart.*

His blue eyes twinkling, he leaned close enough to whisper, "Ask me again later. When we get home. And I promise I'll tell you."

As soon as they got back to the ranch and she put Caitlin down, Jacey went in search of Rafferty.

She found him in the ranch-house living room. A pensive look on his handsome face, he stood, staring at the festively lit tree. Her heart was suddenly thumping so hard she could hear it in her ears.

"So what did you want for Christmas?" she asked.

He turned toward her. Slowly, effortlessly, he closed the distance between them, took both her hands in both of his. Still looking at her as if she was the most beautiful woman on earth, he inclined his head to one side. "It's not really limited to or related to the holiday. What I want is more of a lifelong wish."

She caught her breath at the intensity of his gaze. "And that is...?"

"To love and be loved again," he said, his lips moving across her temple, down her cheek, then hovering above her mouth with tantalizing nearness. "Just like this."

Returning his embrace, Jacey celebrated the fate that had brought her to this ranch, and to him. He parted her lips and slid his tongue into her mouth, kissing her with a need that was sweet and hot and deeply passionate. Jacey wreathed her arms around his neck and kissed him back in a way that had him moaning, too.

He danced her backward, until he had trapped her against the wall and his body. And for that moment in time there was nothing between them except this searing, elemental need. She had never felt this desired. So revered...

A thrill swept through her as he unclasped her bra and molded her breasts with his hands, teasing the nipples into pebble-hard tips. His kiss grew more urgent, and she surged against him, needing so much more. "Rafferty..."

"I know." He placed his hands beneath her hips and scooped her up to waist level, her legs wrapped around his waist. "Nice as that tree is, we've got to get more comfortable...."

He carried her to her bedroom and set her down next to the bed.

"We keep ending up here," she murmured, slipping out of her shoes and skirt.

He shut and locked the door behind them. "Maybe that should tell us something." By the time he'd reached her, his boots and shirt were off, too.

She helped him with his belt and jeans. "Like women who've given birth have a need to assuage certain physical needs and feel desirable again?"

"That, and the fact that the two of us…are meant to be."

Engulfing her with the heat and strength of his body, he lowered his head and delivered another breath-stealing kiss. She trembled, and he kissed her again, shattering whatever reserve she had left.

Her lips parted beneath the pressure of his as his tongue swept her mouth with long sensuous strokes. All the while his hands swept down her body, molding and exploring.

It felt so good to be wanted.

So good to be guided into bed and held against him like this, to have the barriers between them start coming down.

She felt his erection pressing against her, hot and urgent, his heart pounding in his chest.

Need poured out of him, akin to her own.

"I'm through pretending this isn't what I want," he whispered, raining kisses across her face, down her neck, to the shell of her ear. "I want you, Jacey." He tunneled his hands through her hair and claimed her mouth again. "I want you to be mine."

Jacey wanted that, too. So much.

She kissed him back, surrendering the way she never had before. He was so strong and passionate, so undeniably male. "And I want you." She clasped his shoulders and pressed against him.

He grinned. "This time of year, everyone gets their wish."

He slid down her body, kissing the hollow of her stomach, stroking the insides of her thighs. Then he loved her more intimately still, until she was awash in pleasure, shuddering. Until there was no more doubt how much they needed each other, needed this. She lifted her hips, letting him know, without a doubt, it was time.

Kissing her slowly, he edged her knees even farther apart and eased into her. And then she was moaning again, moving against him—with him—her body taking up the timeless rhythm that seemed created just for the two of them. What few boundaries still existed between them dissolved. Pleasure rushed through her as he possessed her tenderly. Feelings triumphed as they moved toward a single goal, savoring the release.

LONG MOMENTS PASSED as they lay tangled together, their intertwined bodies exhausted, yet still eager for more. They had too little time alone, Rafferty thought fiercely. That was going to have to change.

He knew Jacey wasn't ready to deal with the ramifications of their coupling, but he couldn't keep pretending this was only a temporary fling, meant to stem the rising tide of estrogen and need within her. Not when he knew it was so much deeper.

The truth was, Jacey and her baby had brought him back to life.

He would always grieve the loss of his wife and child, but now he was ready to move on.

To experience love again. With Jacey.

He wanted to be more to her than what he was now—friend and part-time lover. A helluva lot more. And he sensed she wanted that, too, even if she wasn't quite ready to admit it.

In the meantime…

He rolled so she was on top of him and began to make love to her once again.

They had this.

Chapter Twelve

"That's the fourth call you've had this morning," Curly teased early Monday morning.

Jacey flushed and continued passing around a second round of buttermilk biscuits, crisp sausage patties and cream gravy—a stick-to-your-ribs breakfast the cowboys could never get enough of.

"I bet I know why they're calling the bunkhouse," Stretch ventured.

"The other ranches want to steal Jacey away from us," Gabby stated unhappily.

"You're getting offers for other chef jobs, aren't you?" Curly added.

Red looked upset. "Is that why the Broken Saddle Ranch called you?"

"I was hoping it was just for your potato-salad recipe," Hoss said.

"And that chocolate-peppermint sheet cake," Rafferty praised.

"You really did the Lost Mountain Ranch proud with the dishes you brought to the Christmas rodeo," Eli said.

The eyes of every cowboy at the bunkhouse table mirrored the same sentiment.

"Thank you." Jacey didn't know when she had received

more compliments, or enjoyed her work so much. Which made the idea of going back to a property-management position all the less appealing. Puttering around the ranch kitchen, trying out new recipes, perfecting old ones, did not even feel like work. It felt like fun... Yet she knew she couldn't stay here and not fall even harder for the elusive rancher. And since she knew she needed love to be happy...

"So, are they trying to steal you away?" Stretch persisted.

Noting that Rafferty looked equally worried, Jacey waved off the concern of the cowboys. She tried not to wonder whether Rafferty was concerned about the loss of a chef or his secret lover. Or both. "I've had a few inquiries," she admitted reluctantly. "I've told them I'm not interested in going to another ranch."

A collective sigh of relief was heard. "Well, thank heavens for that," Hoss said, patting his ample belly. "You've got us spoiled, Jacey."

Another murmur of assent followed.

Guilt swept through her. Conflicted, she turned to Rafferty.

"I hate to break it to you, fellas," he said, "but Jacey isn't going to be staying here indefinitely."

Eli looked at Rafferty. "Unless one of us can convince her otherwise," he said meaningfully.

Ignoring his father's less-than-subtle hint, Rafferty continued, "Jacey has been looking for another position in her field all along. She's even locked up an interview in Austin right after Christmas."

Faces fell. The room reverberated with disappointment.

Rafferty was only speaking the truth. So why, Jacey wondered, did it suddenly feel as if she'd been stabbed in the heart? She plastered a reassuring smile on her face. "I told you-all the way it was from the beginning," she reminded gently. "I only agreed to take this job through the Christmas holiday."

"Yeah, b-but we figured…" Curly stammered, looking like a kid who'd just had his puppy taken away.

Suddenly, Jacey felt like crying, too. She told herself it was a natural reaction to disappointing people she had come to care deeply for. And not the prospect of leaving the only man who had ever made love to her as completely and thoroughly as Rafferty had. Physical passion…one-sided romantic love…was no reason to upend a life. Or trade a sophisticated existence in the city for down-home camaraderie on an isolated ranch—even if it was one of the most beautiful places on earth.

She looked at Rafferty, wishing once again he would rescue her.

Once again, it seemed an emotional wall was up between them, that he was hiding whatever it was he was feeling, from everyone close to him—including her.

"I think what the fellas are trying to say is, it's just not going to be the same around here without you," Rafferty concluded matter-of-factly. And that, it seemed, was that.

"NO DISRESPECT, boss, but was that the best you can do?" Gabby demanded.

Hoss ripped out a damaged section of barbed wire. "Yeah. We don't want Jacey to leave."

Curly hammered in a new metal fence post, to replace the one that had been bent. "She's the best thing that ever happened to this ranch."

Red picked up debris. "Maybe you should offer her a big raise."

"At the very least a huge Christmas bonus," Stretch said,

attaching wire to the post. "Chefs like her do not come along every day."

They were telling him? Rafferty knew Jacey was one in a million. In so many ways that went far beyond her ability to wield a spatula and a frying pan. She brought energy and good cheer to every room she entered. The care she put into her cooking made everyone feel appreciated. Comforted. Like every day was worthwhile. For the first time in a long time, Rafferty found himself happy to get up in the morning, reluctant to go to bed.

"It's not that simple, guys," he said finally. *I made love to her. Allowed myself to begin to depend on her, and let my feelings for her complicate a situation that should have remained simple....*

"Then suppose you explain it to us," Gabby said, looking irritated.

Rafferty went back to the pick-up truck for another roll of wire as a brisk December wind blew across the canyon. Briefly, he turned his attention to the granite mountain rising in the distance.

"She's a city girl," he stated grimly, recalling what trouble that had gotten him into with Angelica. She'd given up her chosen profession, too, to be with him...and been miserable.

Curly yanked off his gloves and gulped down a bottle of water. "If you're talking about the fact Jacey didn't have the right clothes to wear at the Christmas rodeo, whose fault was that?" he asked.

Red agreed. "You didn't exactly give her much notice."

"Yeah," Hoss concurred. "She probably would have gone shopping for something more appropriate to wear if she'd known about it in advance."

"Besides which, I thought she looked real pretty," Stretch said.

"She does know how to two-step," Curly added.

"Yeah. It was real sweet of her to honor each one of us with a dance," Hoss said shyly.

Red complained, "Although some of us hogged her time and attention Saturday night."

All eyes turned to Rafferty.

"Hey, can I help it if I'm a better dancer than the rest of you-all?" Rafferty said, trying to lighten the mood.

A harrumph echoed through the field.

"At least tell us you'll give her a better bonus and you'll give it to her early so she can get it in her head that it might be a good idea for her to stay on," Stretch advised.

"Yeah. We really, really, *really* want her around, boss," Curly said.

They weren't the only ones, Rafferty thought.

Unfortunately, Jacey had other ideas. When dinner was over, and Caitlin had been put down in her bassinet, Jacey asked to speak to him and his dad in the study.

They met her there. She brought a pot of decaf coffee and a plate of the homemade gingerbread cookies she had served the cowboys for dessert that evening. "First of all, I want you both to know I am not going to take a job with a competing ranch, or even consider one, no matter what the offer."

Eli nodded. "We appreciate that."

"Even as we realize," Rafferty said, trying to be fair, "that it's a free market and you're entitled to go wherever you have the best opportunity."

Jacey studied him briefly, no emotion readily identifiable in her eyes. She looked back at his dad. "I know that, but I just don't think it would be right, particularly when you took me in and gave me a job and a place to stay when I had no other options."

"Just promise us you'll at least give us a chance to match any offer you would consider," Eli said. "Because we realize you have a fiscal responsibility to your daughter and yourself."

"I will." Jacey avoided Rafferty's gaze and kept her attention solely on his father. "Although like I said, it's not going to be necessary, because I'm still looking for a job in my field. But until I do secure a property management job that feels right, I would like to stay on here, even as I try to find a suitable replacement for myself. Speaking of which, that's why I called you here. We had a number of applicants to our online ad over the weekend, and more today, and some of them are very interesting. I thought you might want to take a look at their résumés. See what you think."

She handed Rafferty and Eli duplicate copies of twelve applicants.

"There were actually a few more, but I weeded them out. For instance, given the cowboys' reaction to Chinese takeout last week, I really didn't think a guy with seven years' experience in Asian eateries was a good match."

Rafferty and Eli chuckled. "You're right there. It's Tex-Mex and southwestern-style comfort food all the way around here."

Jacey relaxed slightly. "I'm thinking the best thing might be to invite at least a couple of the top contenders out to the ranch and let them cook a meal for the guys and see if it's a good fit. Only one of these people is available immediately, but this way, should that job I'm up for in Austin turn out to be a good fit, you would hopefully already have someone lined up. Even if the person you pick can't start till later."

"When did you want to do this?" Eli asked.

Never, Rafferty thought fiercely.

Jacey smiled. "How about Wednesday—if I can get the guy who's available immediately to come out?"

RAFFERTY WAITED a decent interval of time, then tracked Jacey down in the kitchen, where she was shaping sugar-cookie dough into Christmas bells. Not sure how much time they would have to talk privately, he got straight to the point. "I thought you weren't all that interested in the Austin job." He had taken great comfort in that.

Jacey inclined her head to one side. "When I called this morning to tell them that I didn't feel university students and a baby were a particularly good mix, they offered me a shot at something else in a high-rise across from the state capitol. The downside to that is the job isn't available until May first—they just want something set up now."

Rafferty wanted Jacey to succeed in whatever she did. He just didn't want to lose her in the process. He lounged against the counter where she was working. "Would you be able to take Caitlin to work with you?"

"No." She wrapped the rolls of shaped dough in plastic and slid them into the refrigerator.

She lifted out a stainless-steel mixing bowl and carried it over to the counter.

"But since everything at that property is done by advance appointment and financial prescreening only, I should be able to get sitters to watch Caitlin when I'm meeting with residents. They said there is a lot of paper pushing with that job, and I could do all that at my leisure—in my apartment on my computer—as long as I get it done."

Rafferty watched as she formed teaspoonsful of chilled chocolate dough into balls, and then dipped them in confectioner's sugar. "So you're going up there for an interview."

Jacey arranged the cookie dough on a baking sheet. "On the twenty-sixth of December, yes."

Rafferty studied the smudge of flour in her shiny brown hair.

He erased the powder with the pad of his thumb. "Want company? Someone to watch over Caitlin while you interview?"

Jacey looked up at him, the air between them charged with all the things they had left unsaid the last time they had made love. Things she seemed no more eager to get into now. "Don't, Rafferty," she said in a low voice. "This situation is complicated enough."

It didn't have to be. Rafferty put his hands on her shoulders and turned her to face him. He knew how it felt to be afraid the passion was too wonderful to last. He felt that way now. The difference was, he wasn't going to let his own uncertainty get in the way of what they could have, if only they were steadfast enough to stay the course.

"I want to be alone with you," he told her.

She yearned for further intimacy, too. He could see it in her gaze, feel it in the response of her body next to his.

He lowered his head and their lips met. As if on cue, the baby monitor on the kitchen counter crackled. Caitlin let out a cry. She drew back as the single cry turned into a lusty yell. "I've got to nurse Caitlin. We'll talk more tomorrow…I promise."

Only they didn't talk in the morning. About that, or anything else. Caitlin was unusually fussy and Jacey went off to tend to her while the men ate their breakfast buffet style.

When Rafferty walked into the bunkhouse that evening after his shower, the men were already gathered around Jacey and the baby, paying both the homage they deserved.

Rafferty watched from the fringes of the activity.

There was no denying it. Jacey and baby Caitlin had brought joy to the bunkhouse, the sense that with the two of them there, it would feel like Christmas all year-round. The only problem was, Rafferty mused, how to get them to stay on Lost Mountain Ranch for more than just another week.

'Cause when Jacey and Caitlin left, he knew it was going to feel as if his heart was breaking all over again.

IT TOOK JACEY FOREVER to get Caitlin rocked to sleep that evening. Part of it was the excitement in the bunkhouse. The men had outdone themselves, trying to get her baby girl to smile and coo and bat her long lashes at them. And Caitlin had proved herself up to the challenge as she basked in the adoration of the cowboys.

Caitlin was so *used* to being entertained for long periods every evening and first thing every morning, in fact, that Jacey wondered how her daughter was going to react when she didn't have an admiring coterie of males, ready to grant her very wish.

Just as Jacey wondered how she would react when Rafferty was no longer available to pay her the attention *she* couldn't seem to do without.

But, Jacey sighed, that was not her most pressing problem tonight....

"Something wrong?" a low male voice reverberated in the open doorway to Jacey's bedroom.

Heart racing at the familiar sound, Jacey looked up from where she sat cross-legged in the center of her bed, laptop computer in front of her. "You might say that."

Rafferty ambled closer. She shoved aside the memory of his naked form stretched out next to hers, in this very bed. She did not need to be thinking about warm male skin and evocative lips and hands when she had a fast-approaching deadline to meet and online commerce to arrange. It wasn't like her to be so behind on her shopping. But then, normally, she didn't have a man like Rafferty distracting her.

"Maybe I can help," he said casually.

She regarded him facetiously and quipped, "That all

depends. Can you make a garlic press, a corn stripper, an olive pitter, an avocado slicer and a lemon and lime squeezer magically appear?"

Finally, she'd thrown him off his game.

He blinked. "A...what?"

Jacey patted the mattress beside her, indicating he was welcome to sit down if he wanted. "I finally figured out what I want to get my sister for Christmas."

"Ah." The mattress shifted as it accepted his weight. "All the stuff you just mentioned."

"Right." Jacey pushed away another onslaught of erotic memory. "The problem is, those things are generally only carried by specialty stores. It's no problem to find a kitchen boutique in the city—they're all over the place—but the closest ones to this ranch are in towns that are at least four hours away."

"I see your problem," he said.

Jacey drew a deep, bracing breath. "So, I went online and tried to order them from the Web sites of the two biggest stores in the country, and guess what, they're out of stock until February."

"You could always give her an I.O.U. and a card."

"No. I am determined to track down what I need and make this work."

A wail went up from the adjoining bedroom.

Jacey sighed. "I just put Caitlin down fifteen minutes ago. She's been fed and changed and bathed and rocked."

Times like this—although admittedly few and far between thus far—made her wonder how she was going to manage on her own.

Thankfully, Rafferty seemed to understand even the most devoted mommy occasionally needed backup. "Want me to get her?" he asked gently.

Trying not to think how wonderful it would be to have

Rafferty as Caitlin's daddy, instead of just her lover, Jacey took comfort in his presence instead. "Would you mind walking her around a little bit and just patting her on the back until I finish this?"

RAFFERTY HAD, in fact, been hoping he would be asked to hang out with Jacey and Caitlin for the evening. "No problem," he said.

When he came back with Caitlin snuggled contentedly in his arms, Jacey was on her cell phone, talking to a clerk. She had a pencil stuck in her dark hair, just next to her ponytail, a determined expression on her face.

As usual in the evenings, she had changed her nicer clothing for a pair of black jersey lounge pants and a button-up, long-sleeved T-shirt, worn open at the throat. Her feet were encased in cozy wool socks that coordinated with the red of her shirt and the black of her pants. "Okay, I'll hold, thanks." She stretched out her legs on either side of the computer and wiggled her toes. "The Kitchen Things store in El Paso is going to see if they have any of the items in stock."

While Rafferty tried not to notice the sexy V of her legs, she went back to listening. "You do, really? Three of them? Thank you…! Any idea who would be most likely to have the rest?" Totally caught up in what she was doing, Jacey grabbed her paper and pen.

Forty-five minutes later, Caitlin was asleep on Rafferty's shoulder, and Jacey was finally done with her shopping.

Cheeks flushed with victory, she pantomimed she was ready for her baby.

Rafferty wished he didn't have to give up the child. He could have held and comforted her forever. But he knew it was important to get the infant settled while she was still deep in sleep, if they didn't want Caitlin to wake again.

A transfer was made, with only slight difficulty. Rafferty watched, his heart full, as Jacey carried the softly snoozing infant back to the nursery and tucked her in once again.

Returning, Jacey did a little Snoopy dance. "I got Mindy everything she's wanted for a long time. All I have to do is drop by the customer-service desks of three different kitch-enware stores when I get to El Paso on the twenty-seventh, pick them up, take them back to her place and wrap them."

This, Rafferty thought, was what exasperated him about knickknacks in general and the holidays in particular. "That's a lot to go through for a lemon and lime squeezer."

Jacey wrinkled her nose at him and took down her hair. "Clearly, you do not understand the value of specialty kitchen tools," she accused, running her fingers through her hair.

Rafferty tore his gaze from the silky strands falling across her shoulders. "Okay, explain it," he commanded.

Oblivious of the effect she was having on him, Jacey went back to the bed and shifted her computer onto her lap. She scrolled back to a photo as she talked. "The corn stripper takes the kernels off quick as you please and the kernels stay inside the little compartment instead of flying all over the place."

Rafferty tried, but could not be impressed.

She sighed and rolled her eyes in humorous derision. "Clearly, you've never tried to cut corn off the cob."

Rafferty spread his hands and sauntered closer, glad for another chance to tease her. He liked seeing the playful light come back into her emerald eyes. "Why do that if you can pick it up and eat it right off the cob?"

"Because if you want to cook with fresh corn kernels you

have to cut them off the cob first, and it is a messy and difficult job," she explained.

"Oh."

"Same with pitting olives. And the same tool for that can also be used on cherries."

"That's good to know."

She tilted her head, apparently realizing she was not preaching to the choir. "You don't care."

Rafferty shrugged. "I like to see you happy."

Jacey stood and came closer, in a drift of baby-clean scent. "The thing is," she said even more seriously, "tools like that belong in every kitchen."

"Did you check with Callahan Mercantile and Feed in Summit? They're the biggest retailer around and carry a lot of specialty items."

"For camping and ranching. Not cooking."

"Ah."

"Hannah—the proprietress—was very helpful, though. She told me she has the same problem whenever she needs something not carried around here."

"Maybe you should open a kitchenware and cookbook shop in town then."

"Believe me, I would love to do that, but I can't take on a risky venture like that, now that I have Caitlin to care for."

"Maybe it's not as much of a risk as you think, given how hard it is to find anything like what you've described."

Her eyes clouded over. "I know it's a good idea."

"But...?"

"I'm just not comfortable with putting everything on the line like that financially, not when I have a baby counting on me to support us."

RAFFERTY SPENT a restless night and awakened feeling as if he got up on the wrong side of the bed. His mood was not improved by the increasing merriment in the bunkhouse. There was Christmas music playing on the stereo in the main room at 7:00 a.m. Lights twinkling on the tree. Laughter, good cheer and pancakes in the shape of *reindeer.* Not quite the ambience he would have expected, given that the ranch was soon going to be losing the best thing that had ever happened to it. Unless he figured out how to make Jacey happy enough to stay on.

Meanwhile, the cowboys were busy with some sort of plan of their own. Stretch took the lead, announcing as soon as the dishes were done, "Uh, Jacey, we, uh, need your station wagon for the next day or two, depending."

"On what?" Jacey asked.

"Santa Claus," Curly quipped. "Seems like he might need a little head start this year."

"Now you've really got me curious," Jacey said with a smile.

"Well, don't be too curious," Gabby warned, "because we all want you to be surprised."

"Any idea what they're up to?" Jacey asked Rafferty after the bunkhouse emptied out, and it was just him and her and the baby once again.

"None." Except he was sure it was some way to induce her to stay on as ranch chef.

She threw a blanket over her shoulder and sat down to nurse. "Any guesses then?"

Rafferty shrugged. It had never bothered him to be left out of Christmas preparations. Until now. "They might be having your station wagon detailed for you."

She bit her lip, thinking. "But it would just get dusty again when they were driving it back here."

"Good point."

"So what could it be?" Jacey wondered, mystified.

Rafferty did not know. What he did realize was how excited Jacey was getting at the thought of receiving a Christmas present from the guys. And that, in turn, left him in the ditch, because he had no idea what he should get her. Casually, he turned a chair around and sank into it backward. Folding his arms across the top, he said, "I was thinking I'd like to get Caitlin a gift." He figured that was a good place to start.

Jacey's eyes sparkled. "Would that be you, Rafferty Evans, *participating in Christmas?*"

She had to know she was wearing him down with her nonstop holiday cheer. He feigned nonchalance. "It could be a happy-you're-seven-weeks-old-and-doing-so-well-kind-of-gift."

"Mmm, hmm." She did not look convinced.

Self-consciously, he tried again. "So what do you think she might like?" He really wanted to do this right.

"A play gym."

Rafferty paused. "To climb on outside?"

Jacey shifted the baby to her other breast, the blanket covering her slipping only slightly. "No. It's a quilted mat that you put on the floor, and it has these contraptions that go up in the air, over the baby, with toys hanging down that the baby can watch and touch. She may be a tad young for it, but I'd really like her to have one."

"What does she need?"

"Isn't that enough?"

Rafferty shrugged, not sure he could explain how important it was to him that Jacey and Caitlin not want for anything. "My dad and the fellas might want to get her something, too," he fibbed.

"I think they already have, Rafferty."

Once again, beaten to the punch.

"But thank you for thinking of my baby girl. I appreciate it."

Silence fell. Aware all over again just how empty his life had been up to now, Rafferty asked, "Do you have plans for the day?"

"Yes," Jacey said mysteriously. "I do."

Longing welled inside him. "Want to share them?"

Jacey shook her head. "It's a secret."

"WHAT PUT A THORN in your paw?" Eli asked two hours later.

Rafferty paced the halls of the ranch house. Today being one of the days he had ascribed to compensation time off for the hired hands, he had hoped to spend it with Jacey and Caitlin.

Instead, she had run off to heaven knows where—taking his dad's pickup and her baby—while he was left here, trying to fill the empty hours by working on the spring sale catalog.

Meanwhile…even his father seemed to have gotten in the spirit. Eli was in the kitchen, singing Christmas carols, while clumsily wrapping presents he had bought for everyone on the ranch.

Rafferty examined the talking teddy bear his father had purchased for Caitlin. It was really cute. "That apron for Jacey?" Blue denim, it had Best Chef in Texas embroidered across the front.

"Got one of the ladies at the barbecue last weekend to make it for me. They were sure she'd like it because it'll protect her fancy clothes from cooking stains."

Rafferty had never noticed Jacey getting anything on herself, no matter what she was making. "It's a nice gift," he said grudgingly.

"Too bad you're not into Christmas," his father said. "Otherwise, you might be having a little fun, getting into the spirit, yourself."

"I'm fine," Rafferty said stubbornly. Although it was getting harder and harder to defend his Ebenezer Scrooge mentality. Lost Mountain Ranch hadn't been this lively in years.

"Since you're not intending to buy Jacey anything…"

Who said he wasn't? Rafferty fumed.

Eli finished sagely, "Maybe you could do something that demonstrates how much Jacey and her little girl have come to mean to you, instead."

Chapter Thirteen

Rafferty was sitting in the middle of the nursery, antique crib parts all around him, when Jacey walked in with Caitlin. A quizzical expression on her face, she set the baby on the diaper changing pad on the bed. "What's going on here?" she asked.

"It was supposed to be a Chr—" Rafferty stopped himself just in time, correcting himself "—a surprise."

She grinned at what he had almost said and went about diapering the baby. "Well, you accomplished that, all right."

"I thought you might want Caitlin sleeping in more than the bassinet—given how big she's getting. So I dug this out of the storeroom and cleaned it up, only to find out that there are no instructions as to how to put the parts together so the side rail will move up and down. Plus, I'm not sure where the linens are to fit the crib, if we still have any, that is. My mother may have given them away years ago. She just held on to the crib because she wanted her grandchildren to use it."

"I can see why." Finished, Jacey put the soiled diaper in the pail and went to wash her hands. She returned to get Caitlin, then ran a hand lovingly over the solid cherry end board. "It's very beautiful. But you didn't have to go to all this trouble, Rafferty. The bassinet in here, and the Pack 'n Play over in the bunkhouse are just fine."

For now, Rafferty thought. "The point is, we can do better by you."

Jacey sent him a grateful glance. "You and your dad have done plenty to see that we're comfortable." She smoothed the tufted curls on the top of her daughter's head.

Figuring he would have to look on the Internet to see if he could find instructions for this crib, or a similarly designed one, Rafferty stood.

Aware it had been too long since he had held Jacey's little girl, he ambled closer and held out his hands. She leaned toward him and Jacey handed Caitlin over.

"Do you know what time the fellas are due back this evening?" She glanced at the clock on the bureau, saw it was four o'clock.

Rafferty tucked his index finger in Caitlin's fist. "They're staying in El Paso tonight."

"El Paso?" Jacey repeated, as if not sure she'd heard right.

Rafferty lifted Caitlin's fist to his lips for a gentle, affectionate kiss. He didn't know if it was that he had helped bring this little girl into the world, or that she was Jacey's daughter, but he loved her every bit as much as he would have loved the child he had lost. His feelings for her mother were equally strong.

Realizing Jacey was waiting for his answer, Rafferty explained, "The guys had some big holiday errand to do. And they weren't going to be done until sometime tomorrow."

Jacey sighed with frustration. "So I guess that means my Volvo station wagon is still with them?"

With his free hand, Rafferty tucked a strand of Jacey's hair behind her ear. "I would imagine so."

"You don't think they've gotten it in their heads to have it painted a different shade of red or something, do you?" she asked worriedly.

Rafferty hoped not. Vehicle color was such an individual thing. "I'm sure it's nothing that elaborate," he said. Although they wouldn't have had to drive the car for four hours to have it professionally washed and waxed—they could have it detailed in Summit, or Fort Stockton. The closest Volvo dealership, however, was in El Paso. But what could they be doing there?

Rafferty thought a moment, surprised by how interested he was getting in all the gift-giving secrecy, and all because of Jacey.

She looked at him, as if hoping for some essential clue. Finally, he said, "The hubcaps on it are kind of plain. Guys like fancy hubcaps."

Jacey propped her hips against the bureau. "Well, whatever they are doing," she said at last, "I am sure it's with a lot of love...so I know I'll like it."

Rafferty was sure of that, too.

The hired hands revered Jacey too much to do anything less than top-notch. Which was undoubtedly why they'd felt it necessary to go all the way to El Paso.

"So it's just the three of us for dinner tonight, then?" Jacey said.

"Two," Rafferty corrected. "Dad went to Marfa to see some old friends."

Jacey took a moment to digest that. "Does he normally have so many social invitations?"

"During the holidays, yes. It's well known that I don't have a lot of yuletide spirit." At least up till now, Rafferty added silently. "Christmas has always meant a lot to my dad. People know he really misses my mom at this time of year, so they include him in their own festivities and he's happy to go."

"Whereas you..."

"Generally prefer not to." Although, Rafferty thought, that

too was beginning to change. He wouldn't mind taking Jacey and Caitlin both out a lot more. Publicly claiming them as his. Although that was going to take some careful handling. He didn't want to do anything that would cause Jacey to be any more skittish than she already was by pushing her into something she was not ready for. When she signaled to him that she was ready to take the next step, he would go for it. No holds barred.

Lost in her own thoughts, Jacey cuddled Caitlin close, her expression as tender as he knew his had been just moments before, when he had held the infant. "Any requests then?"

Yes, Rafferty thought, a solid night of lovemaking followed by breakfast in bed—served by him to the lovely woman in his life. Thinking it might be a little presumptuous of him to say so, however, he merely shrugged. "Whatever is easiest to prepare. I can even put together some sandwiches if you want. Or if you want to go back into town, I'll take you out for dinner."

Jacey waved off the offer of another two hours' commuting time, just for the privilege of eating in a restaurant. "That's okay. I don't mind doing my job. But I do have a favor to ask."

Rafferty caught her as she passed, and gathered her close. "Name it."

Jacey smiled. "Hold Caitlin while I bring in my presents...? And no peeking! I don't want anyone seeing anything I bought before I wrap it." She tapped the center of his chest with her fingertip. "And that includes you, cowboy."

He chuckled at her indignant expression. "Why not?"

She transferred the baby to him. Then eased away from him, the sight of her back as tantalizing as her front. "Because I don't know if you can keep a secret."

He flashed a devil-may-care grin. "Seems to me I've been doing a pretty good job so far."

Jacey turned around and rolled her eyes in exasperation. "About something else besides the fact we've hooked up," she said, no more able to contain her happiness than he could.

Unable to help himself, he nodded at the vehicle in the driveway and prompted, "So I guess that means there's something for me in there?"

Jacey wrinkled her nose at him playfully. "Not telling."

Rafferty watched Jacey turn and sashay out to the pick-up truck she'd borrowed, then carried Caitlin into the living room to wait, out of sight.

Her eyes were immediately drawn to the Christmas tree, which looked a little plain without the lights twinkling, so he turned them on.

Caitlin gurgled in delight and made a clumsy attempt to reach for a branch.

Rafferty moved closer. Still cuddling her close, he guided her tiny fist to the fragrant green branch and watched as she explored it tentatively then held on tight. Transfixed, she studied the decorations.

"You look content" a soft voice spoke behind him.

Rafferty turned. Jacey stood there, hair windblown, cheeks and lips pink. "I still have part of a bottle of breast milk left. If you want to feed her, I can go ahead and get some supper on for us."

Nothing, Rafferty thought, would please him more.

She warmed the bottle and shook it well. Rafferty sat in a chair in the kitchen, while Jacey puttered around the room, expertly throwing a meal together.

Rafferty had never considered himself a homebody—he preferred being out on the range. But being here with Jacey and Caitlin, in the house where he'd grown up, he felt more content and at peace than he had in a very long time. And it was all due to the woman in front of him, and the joy she and her baby girl had brought into his life.

"You're really good with babies," Jacey noted when Caitlin had finished her bottle and fallen asleep with her cheek pressed against his shoulder, one tiny arm encircling his neck.

Jacey came closer and just stood there, savoring the sweetness of the moment, just as he was. She plucked the digital camera off the kitchen counter and snapped a few pictures of her daughter sleeping contently in Rafferty's arms.

"Had a lot of practice?" she continued as casually as if they were just friends, instead of a whole lot more.

Rafferty shifted the infant gently so Jacey could get a better image of her daughter's cherubic features. "Just this little darlin'," he murmured.

With a sigh, Jacey returned the camera to the counter. "You should be a father someday."

There was only one child he could see himself fathering at the moment. The little girl in his arms. Rafferty returned his gaze to Jacey's. His desire to protect the two of them growing by leaps and bounds, he asked quietly, "Have you given any more thought to my offer to be her godfather?" *To having me in your lives permanently?*

"Yes, I have," Jacey said, looking as at peace with her decision as he wanted her to be. "If you're still willing, Rafferty, I'd like that very much."

IN LINE WITH his new responsibility, Rafferty took another stab at putting the crib frame together after the dinner dishes were done. While he worked, Jacey embarked on another evening of yuletide baking.

When that was done, he got on the Internet and ordered a new mattress for the crib, along with several changes of linens that were suitable for a baby girl.

He paid extra to have it delivered by Christmas Eve.

Suddenly inspired, he went back online and added a few toys and a nursing cushion for Jacey that was supposed to make her more comfortable than the bed pillow she was currently using.

Then he got to thinking about the red cowgirl boots she had admired in the western-wear store. He found a pair of her shoes and checked out her size, then called the store and put a hold on a pair of those, too.

As long as he was doing that, he ordered his father a new suede jacket with a sheepskin lining, and a hat to go with it. Then he purchased a dozen new movies on DVD for the hired hands.

He didn't know what it was this year.

Maybe he was making up for lost time…but he couldn't stop shopping.

Any more, apparently, than Jacey could stop baking sugary holiday treats.

He followed the delicious aroma. She was standing at the kitchen table, assembling sheets of precut gingerbread with thick white icing.

His gut tightened with emotion.

She looked over at him with a shy smile, knowing full well how much this meant to him, both in the past, and especially now. She slathered snow on the roof, let it drip down the eaves. "Want to help me decorate?" she asked softly.

Inundated by happy memories of Christmases past, and hope for all the holidays of the future, he nodded. "Sure." Adopting her too-cool tone, he picked up a few gumdrops and placed them around the base of the house. She framed the windows and doors with red licorice.

"You even got peppermint sticks." Pleased, he anchored two in the icing on either side of the snow surrounding the house.

"Of course." She reached into the pocket of her apron and produced a foil-wrapped Santa and Mrs. Claus and eight chocolate reindeer. She made a comical face that invited teasing one-upmanship. "You have to know there isn't anything I wouldn't do to see you celebrate Christmas at long last."

He shook his head, loving the mischief in her eyes as much as he loved everything she did and said. "All this…just to win our bet?" He wrapped his arms around her waist and drew her close.

She shook her head and splayed her hands across his chest. "Just to see you happy again," she corrected. The mischief in her eyes faded, replaced by something even more intoxicating. "As happy as you should be," she whispered, slanting her face up to his.

"Well," he drawled, tenderness unlike anything he had ever felt filling his heart, "if that's what you want…"

"Oh, it is." She lifted her lips closer still, kissing him with a hunger and a yearning he not only understood but felt himself. Whether she wanted to admit it or not, Jacey had been his destiny ever since the first time they had made love. He saw it in the way she looked at him when they were alone, and even when they weren't. He felt it in the way she responded to him, opening her mouth and drawing his tongue deep inside, in the way she clung to him and surged against him. There was no fighting this, he thought, as desire raged through him. Unable to get enough of her, he kissed her with an intensity that took their breath away, until she surrendered to his will, as surely as he gave in to hers.

Sweeping her up into his arms, he carried her to her bedroom. Satisfaction unfurled within him as he set her down next to the bed. His own body shaking with the effort it took to suppress his pressing needs, he let her go long enough to strip down to his skin.

Her eyes widened at the sight of his arousal, and then their lips came together once again.

Slowly, deliberately, he undressed her, too. Delighting in the sight of her, he took his time uncovering every supple curve. Kissing and touching, paying homage, until the remnants of past heartaches and disappointments faded away, and there was just the joy they found in being together the way they were meant to be.

He caressed her creamy breasts and rosy nipples, going lower still, until her skin was so hot it burned and her hips rose instinctively to meet him.

They dropped onto the bed. He lay astride her and parted her legs. Their mouths meshed again as he touched and rubbed and stroked. She caressed him in turn, taking him to new heights. She ran her hands over his chest. Shifting onto her side, she moved closer, until skin met skin and her thighs moved with delicious friction against his. He shifted, so she was lying on top of him. Running her hands up and down his arms, she kissed him, not the tentative exploratory kisses of their initial courtship, but deep, urgent kisses that rocked him to his soul.

Jacey sighed as he found a way to slip his hands between their bodies and touch her there. He was making her want, making her need. A hunger unlike any she had ever felt built inside. Awash in sensation, she closed her eyes and arched against him. Seconds later, she fell apart in his hands, and then he was shifting her back down again. And they became one. Gloriously, wonderfully one.

Her body took up the same timeless rhythm as his. He took

her higher still, going slow, going deep, until she heard the soft, whimpering sounds in her throat, until his body was shuddering, too, and all was lost in a blinding explosion of heat.

Together, they drifted back down. Sated with love, damp with sweat, Jacey collapsed against his chest. She could feel the thundering of his heart, in tempo to hers, even as she nestled against him contentedly and rested her head on his shoulder.

Luxuriating in all that was Rafferty, Jacey lifted her head and looked into his eyes. They might not have said the words yet, but she knew she loved him, and for her—for now—that was Christmas enough.

RAFFERTY WOKE ALONE, in his own bed. Once again, he and Jacey had been forced to part company and had spent the night alone. And although he was happy to do whatever needed to be done to protect Jacey's privacy, as well as his own, he was not content with the situation as it was.

He was tired of sneaking around. Tired of hiding his feelings for Jacey. She was the best thing that had ever happened to him. It was past time everyone knew how serious he was about giving Jacey—and Caitlin—the happiness they deserved.

He was still thinking about how to do that when he walked into the kitchen that morning.

Caitlin was sitting in her infant seat, alternately fingering a cloth-covered snap-on rattle in the shape of a rooster, and watching Jacey put the finishing touches on the gingerbread house they had abandoned the night before.

Rafferty helped himself to some coffee, then lounged against the counter, appreciating the sight. "What are your plans for the day?"

Jacey opened a bag of dark green mints. "A little baking. Some gift-wrapping. And the first chef interview."

Rafferty accepted her wordless invitation to plant the sugary discs in the snow in front of one half of the house, while she did the other. "Is he going to cook?"

Finished, Jacey piped a little more icing on top of the shrubbery. "All part of the screening process. Fortunately, the guys will be back by then, so they can sample the food and give their two cents."

He suppressed the need to forget everything else but the chemistry flowing between them. "I hope they're...kind."

She bent to inspect her work. "Why wouldn't they be?"

He moved back reluctantly. "You're a hard act to follow." *And they don't want you to leave any more than I do.*

Jacey straightened abruptly, the soft swell of her breast brushing his biceps. She stepped back. An emotion he couldn't decipher simmered in her eyes. "Don't be silly. This guy has cooked at half a dozen ranches. I'm sure he'll be fine." She paused to lick her lips. "What are you going to do?"

Start securing our future.

He looked at Jacey, then Caitlin, and back again. "I'm going into Fort Stockton."

"For...?"

It wouldn't take much to get it out of him, especially if he kissed her again. Telling himself this was one instance in which timing was everything, Rafferty shrugged. "It's a secret."

An aha! expression crossed her pretty face. "You're beginning to sound like you might have caught the Christmas spirit," she teased.

Rafferty winked. Giving in to the desire that had been building since he had first walked in, he circled his hands around her waist and shifted her against him. "I don't know about that," he said, feeling the soft surrender of her slender body as it molded against his. "You might have to keep working on me."

He cut off whatever else she had been about to say with a soft, persuasive kiss. She had used a mint-flavored mouthwash and it mingled with the sweet taste that was her. He took full advantage of their alone time, foraging her mouth, reminding her of all they had shared the night before. When she moaned, he drew her even more flush against him. He wanted her to feel his hardness, to know how much she aroused him, and he wanted to pleasure her, too. The press of their bodies, the thrust and parry of their tongues, sent a wake-up call to every inch of his body. And Rafferty knew when they did make love again—hopefully very soon—it would be hotter, and more exciting than ever.

Knowing that would have to wait until they could take the time with each other they needed, he let the kiss come to a lazy halt and drew back reluctantly.

Jacey's eyes were soft and misty, her lips dewy. To his immense satisfaction, she looked every bit as turned on as he was.

"You've absolutely got to stop distracting me," Jacey whispered, looking as if she wanted nothing more than to start kissing him again.

Only the happy gurgle of her infant daughter, the shake of a rattle and the sound of a door shutting kept them from doing just that.

Rafferty unhooked his hands from around Jacey's waist and glanced out the window. "Sounds like my dad is back." Eli had been off early, on another Christmas errand.

Jacey playfully tapped his backside. "You better get a move on, cowboy. Don't want to be caught kissing me when there's no mistletoe."

Actually, Rafferty thought, he would. Which was why he had to go to Fort Stockton. It was time he took the next important step in their relationship. Past time, actually.

When he returned, four hours later, the hired hands still weren't back from El Paso. Baffled as to why there was no other vehicle in the driveway—there should have been if the chef applicant was there as scheduled—Rafferty went into the bunkhouse.

It smelled great—thanks to the beef and jalapeño pepper stew simmering in the two big Crock-Pots sitting on the stainless-steel counter—but that was Jacey's recipe.

Wondering what had happened to the chef who was supposed to interview that night, Rafferty headed over to the ranch house. His dad was no help since he was sound asleep on the living-room sofa. Rafferty covered him with an afghan and went in search of Jacey.

He heard her talking to what sounded like her sister as he walked down the hallway toward the bedroom.

His gut tightened as he picked up on the tension of the discourse. "…of course I miss the city…"

Just as Angelica had.

Exasperation colored Jacey's low tone. "I know I said I was only going to be here through Christmas, Mindy…but the guys need me." Jacey sighed. "I just don't feel that I can leave until there is a replacement…. It's not that easy." She paused, and then continued, her voice tight, "I've spent weeks looking for someone who might take the job, and the most likely candidate of all was a no-show today. He bailed when he realized just how far out the ranch is. I'm thinking about rescheduling, or maybe even calling off the interview in Austin on the twenty-sixth…and just staying on the ranch. Everyone here has come to mean a lot to me."

Rafferty's hopes rose.

His hand closed around the gift in his pocket.

Aware this situation was turning out better than he had

dared hope, he peered around the corner of Jacey's bedroom. The door was open. She was surrounded by wrapping paper and presents, and had her back to him. The phone was right next to her, the speaker button glowing red.

Mindy's voice came out of the receiver as loudly as if she were standing there in the room. "It's because of Rafferty Evans, isn't it?"

Jacey ran an aggravated hand through her dark brown hair. "Don't start," she warned.

Mindy continued, like the oft-overbearing big sister she was. "I can't help it. Mom's not here anymore. Someone has to watch out for you."

"I'm a grown woman."

"Whose judgment is apparently all askew."

"I know what I'm doing."

"I know you just had a baby and your hormones are raging. As is your biological need to nest and provide safety for your offspring."

"I can do that on my own!"

"Exactly what I'm trying to tell you!"

Jacey buried her face in her hands and groaned in aggravation.

Mindy persisted. "Let's look at this logically, okay? You've just spent the last ten years working in property management. You've got a fine career going there, but if you step off that track on a whim, it may not be so easy to get back on, particularly since you were more or less let go from your last job."

"I'd still be there if I were willing to leave Caitlin with a sitter all day and I'm not."

"I get that the position at the ranch has served a purpose in the short term, but what about the long term? Is this really what you want for yourself and your daughter?"

"She's happy here."

"And you won't be, not as a ranch employee with no real chance at advancement."

Jacey fell silent.

She still had her back to him, but he could tell she looked miserable.

Guilt filled him anew as he realized he was about to ruin another woman's life by expecting her to give up everything just to be with him. He had never wanted to hurt or constrain Jacey. He wanted to give her the world....

On the phone, Mindy continued, more contritely, "Look, honey, I'm sorry to be so harsh, but you're doing what you always do here. You're allowing yourself to get comfortable in a place where you shouldn't be staying on permanently, just because it's easy and feels good to you now. And in the process, you're severely limiting your own future, and now by extension, your little girl's. What about your dreams? Your hopes? Your aspirations?"

Jacey threw up her hands and sat back in her chair. "I've told you a million times, I don't want to go back to school to get an MBA!"

But Jacey did, Rafferty thought, want to open her own kitchenware and cookbook boutique. She simply did not feel she was financially in a place to take the risk.

"Don't fall into the same old trap and shortchange yourself once again," Mindy pleaded. "Forget about what's best for all those cowboys, and for once in your life, take a risk and do right by you!"

Rafferty walked away as silently as he'd approached.

As much as he did not want to admit it, Mindy was right, he thought sadly. Jacey had not received all she deserved. Not nearly. But that could—and would—change. Starting today.

Chapter Fourteen

"Got a minute?" Jacey asked Rafferty from the study doorway.

Her timing could not have been more perfect. He'd been wanting to see her, too. "For you?" he returned with a grin. "Always." He ushered her in and shut the door behind her.

Because she appeared to be there on business, he guided her to one of the chairs in front of his desk. Then he sat down next to her and turned his chair so they were facing each other. "What's up?"

She held her pen above the clipboard in her hand. "I'm taking requests for the Christmas Eve and Christmas Day menus. I want to make sure everyone gets at least one, if not all, of their favorite things."

Rafferty wasn't surprised Jacey was going all out. She took her cooking very seriously. "Whatever you want to prepare is great." She'd already done so much, for all of them….

Jacey searched his face. "Sure?"

Rafferty nodded as joy washed over him. If everything fell into place as he hoped it would, by this time next year they'd be a real family. He'd have a wife and child to come back to every night. "You've already made a gingerbread house. Assorted cookies…." *Done everything you could to bring me back to life and make all my dreams come true.*

Jacey narrowed her eyes, more eager to please than ever. "There must be something you want," she insisted.

Rafferty took the clipboard and pen from her, set them aside, and shifted her over onto his lap. "There is." He tucked his fingers beneath her chin and stroked his thumbs across her cheeks. She let out a soft exhalation and he kissed her with the promise of the days and nights to come.

Taking both her hands in his, he gazed into her eyes and continued, "I'm giving all the ranch employees their Christmas gifts and bonuses on the twenty-fifth, but I have something for you today."

Emotion glimmered in her pretty eyes. "Does this mean you're actually participating in Christmas?" she asked triumphantly.

Rafferty chuckled. "I think we both know you won that bet a long time ago," he conceded. "So, yes, I am celebrating Christmas this year."

Jacey's face lit up even more. "Your dad is going to be so happy."

Rafferty released his hold on her reluctantly and moved behind his desk. Quickly, he booted up the Summit, Texas, real estate listings on his computer and motioned Jacey over. "There's something I want you to look at." When she rounded the desk, he guided her into the chair and stood behind her.

Jacey's brow furrowed as she studied the screen. She swiveled to look up at him. "Why am I looking at a commercial building on Main Street?"

He turned her chair right back and pointed to a row of photos at the bottom of the computer screen. "Notice that it also has a three-room apartment on the second floor that comes with the lease."

"Okay." She still looked confused.

Rafferty came around the chair to sit on the edge of the desk, facing her. "For your kitchenware and cookbook boutique," he explained.

A troubled look clouded her eyes. "I thought I explained. I don't have the money to start a business right now."

Rafferty nodded. "But I do."

JACEY STARED at Rafferty, her heart thudding uncertainly in her chest. Call her a fool. But she had really been expecting him to do something over-the-top-romantic when it came to celebrating the holiday with her—like propose.

Instead, this…

"It's my Christmas gift to you," Rafferty informed her. He reached into his center desk drawer and handed her an envelope.

Fingers trembling, she looked inside, saw the five figures typed on the personal check and wanted to sink through the floor.

"That'll cover the lease and utilities for one year, and start-up inventory. I figure with the number of tourists that come through Summit, and the lack of other specialty shops in this part of Texas, you ought to do just fine. Especially if you add a mail-order component, the way they've done over at Callahan Mercantile and Feed."

"You've given this a lot of thought," she announced numbly, still feeling a little stunned at the swift way he was booting her and her daughter off the ranch and out of his life.

He appeared sincere. "I want you to get what you want out of life, Jacey. And not be stuck here indefinitely."

That was one way to put it. She gave him a withering look, making no effort at all to hide her hurt over his actions. "So you're easing me out," she concluded, abruptly recalling what the librarian had said.

Watch out for Rafferty Evans. He's left a string of broken hearts from here to Big Bend National Park. I dated him for two months, six years ago. I thought we were getting serious. Next thing I know, he's easing away from me, ever so kindly, the same way he eased away from all his other girlfriends.

It was Rafferty's turn to look confused—but no less determined to see his plan through. "I figured it was what you wanted. Even if you were too considerate to leave us in the lurch. But you don't need to worry about that," he consoled her gallantly. "I had another talk with the chef that was supposed to come out for a trial run yesterday. He said if he could leave the ranch from Friday to Sunday every week he would consider working here temporarily."

It galled her to think how easily he was planning to replace her. "How noble of him."

Her sarcasm was lost on Rafferty.

"If he doesn't work out, we'll find someone to replace him ASAP, Jacey."

This time she couldn't help it—she scoffed. "How noble of *you.*"

Rafferty's lips thinned. "I'm getting the idea you don't like my gift."

Given what she had been planning to bestow on him…? The news that she was committing to the job for as long as they wanted and needed her at the ranch? Their presents to each other were so ironically mismatched it was almost funny. Or would have been, Jacey amended silently, if her heart hadn't ached so very badly.

Figuring she could at least hold on to her pride, Jacey bounded out of the desk chair, all self-reliant energy once again. "No problem," she stated with an inner cheer she could not begin to feel. "Caitlin and I will be out of here on the twenty-sixth—early. And you can replace me right away."

Rafferty caught her wrist before she could complete her escape and reeled her back. Her hip bumped the outside of his knee. "I'm not sure the building will be ready for occupancy by then."

She loathed the way he was still sitting casually on the edge of his desk. But then, his life was not falling apart. Hers was. "I won't be staying," she told him coolly. "I'm going to live with my sister in El Paso until I find another job."

Rafferty blinked in shock. "What about us?"

What about them? It wasn't as if they were going to drag this out indefinitely, even if his lovemaking had made her feel like the most special woman in the world. Jacey shrugged. "Consider me eased out of your life," she said sweetly.

"You're dumping me?" Rafferty asked incredulously.

Jacey folded her arms in front of her. "Consider us dumping each other," she advised levelly, figuring this was the only way to take the high road. "That way, neither of us has to feel guilty."

Rafferty's expression hardened. "This isn't what I want."

Jacey leaned close enough to inhale the brisk, masculine scent of him. "Then what do you want?" she queried, unable to hide her resentment any longer. "Some sort of arrangement where you sneak into town to see me?"

Displeasure hardened the handsome features of his face. "I think we've done enough sneaking around," he concluded. "Don't you?"

Bitterness filled her heart. Why did she never see this coming? When would she ever realize she was about to be excised from a man's life?

"You're right about that. Our sneaking-around days are over!" She marched to the door, yanked it open.

"Jacey…"

She paused in the door of the study, tears stinging her eyes. She held up a staying hand. "You're getting what you want, Rafferty," she told him hoarsely. "Consider my leaving my Christmas gift to you."

Without waiting for a response, she turned around and stormed out.

"BOSS, WE GOT SOMETHING to say to you."

Rafferty looked up from the horse he was saddling. If ever there was a time when he didn't need an employee revolt, it was now. But it looked as if he was about to have one anyway.

"We just found out you're letting Jacey go," Stretch said unhappily.

That was a gross misstatement. "I didn't let her go. She quit."

"Only because you forced her to," Curly countered, "by bringing in some other dude that isn't even willing to cook on weekends, like she is."

"Without her, we're going to go back to starving," Hoss complained.

Rafferty tightened the cinches around his mount's belly. "I hardly think that will be the case," he said with a great deal more ease than he felt.

"Well, we sure won't be happy," Red growled.

Rafferty adjusted the reins, wishing he were already out on the range, riding hell for leather. "And you think I will be?"

Gabby folded his arms. "If you were unhappy, you would do something about it."

"Yeah," Stretch concurred. "We've done our part by helping her out as much as possible and getting her a really great Christmas gift."

Rafferty had seen what the present was. They had gone all

out. Their gift to Jacey showed a lot of thought, as well as genuine concern for her well-being. "She's really going to like that," he said sincerely, willing to give praise where it was due.

"The only thing around here she doesn't like, it would seem, is you, boss," Curly said, scowling.

"We need you to fix this!" Hoss implored.

"Make her stay!" Red pleaded.

Stretch threw up his hands. "Help her understand how much she has changed things around here!"

If Rafferty could…

He hardened his heart against further hurt and disappointment. Forced himself to be reasonable, even if it hurt. "I'm not forcing a city girl to stay on this ranch, fellas. I've already done that, as you may recall. It didn't work out."

"Jacey is no Angelica," Gabby retorted. "No disrespect…"

"None taken. And I know that." Jacey was everything his late wife hadn't been. Loving. Tender. Compassionate. Sensitive. Generous to a fault. The other half of his soul…

"She loves it here." Stretch looked as if he was about to cry.

Rafferty knew how that felt, too.

"She loves us," Curly continued.

She just doesn't love me, Rafferty thought on an inward sigh, not sure how he had landed here when he'd thought he finally had everything, or was about to.

Some of his confusion must have showed, because the next thing Rafferty knew, the cowboys were all commiserating with him, trying to help, rather than simply accuse. "Look, boss, all we know is that everything was fine until she went off to talk to you, and then it wasn't fine anymore, so you must have done something."

He'd never been more generous—and selfless—in his life. Did Jacey think he wanted her to leave? That he wanted to have to drive all the way into town to so much as catch a glimpse of her? Yet he'd made that sacrifice so all her dreams could come true. He shook his head in rueful regret. "All I did was try to give her a Christmas gift. Something I thought she wanted."

"Well, she must not have wanted it," Gabby declared.

No kidding. Rafferty thought with heartfelt regret.

"Give her something else," Hoss urged.

"Something better," Red added.

"The kind of thing all women want," Curly persuaded.

"First of all, Jacey isn't 'all women'," Rafferty lectured the cowboys. She was one of a kind. The most special, incredible woman he had ever met in his entire life.

Stretch threw up his hands. "Then give her something she wants!"

That was the hell of it, Rafferty thought, even more dejected. He hadn't a clue what that might be.

"THANKS FOR AGREEING to go to the grocery store with me," Jacey told Eli as they headed for town in one of the ranch pick-up trucks, with Caitlin in her car seat in the rear passenger seat. She was going to need help getting all the ingredients she would need to cook for the cowboys the next two days.

"No problem. Although I would have thought this was something you would want to do to with Rafferty."

Not anymore, Jacey thought furiously, aware she had never felt more disillusioned and hurt than she did at that moment.

"Is something going on between the two of you?" Eli asked. "Did you quarrel?"

Her emotions in turmoil, Jacey bit her lip. "You might say that. I gave my notice." *But only after he took steps to ease me off the ranch and out of his life.*

"I thought you were happy here."

So had Jacey. She pretended to study the extensive grocery list in her hands. "It's complicated."

"Love usually is."

Jacey shot Rafferty's dad a sharp look.

He tightened his hands on the wheel and spared her an understanding glance. "You think I didn't know? I'd have to be blind not to see the sparks between the two of you. And for the record, Rafferty hasn't been this happy in years."

That's what she had thought. Sighing wistfully, Jacey steeled herself against further heartache. "It was never going to work anyway," she said sadly. For once, the Christmas music on the truck stereo did nothing to lift her sagging spirits.

"Why do you say that?"

Jacey studied the Christmas lights on the houses at the edge of town. "I'm a city girl. I don't ride. Don't even want to learn."

"So? His mother never rode, either. Horses scared her. Same for cattle and any other critters she might come across out on the ranch. The kitchen and home were her domain and she loved every second of it. And Rafferty loved her, as did I."

Jacey took a deep breath and pushed back the tears she felt gathering behind her eyes. "Well, then, I guess I'm not ambitious enough for him."

Eli frowned in disagreement. "How can that be true, given how many different dishes you're going to be making over Christmas, just to ensure that everyone has their favorite food?"

"That's different." It was so much fun it didn't even feel like work.

"Is it? Every other cook we've had—aside from my wife— has set out a very brief, pedestrian menu, and if the hands didn't like it, that was just tough. You go out of your way to cook extraordinary meals."

"But it's not my profession."

"Then maybe it should be."

Jacey didn't want to admit how tempted she was. "I can't continue working on the ranch, and be around Rafferty, knowing he wants me gone." *It would be just too painful.*

Eli turned into the grocery-store parking lot and began looking for a space. It wasn't easy—the lot was full. "So you're just going to give up because it's easy?" He finally eased into a space.

Despair filled Jacey's voice. "You can't make someone love you." *As much as you might want to do so.*

"Nor can you stop on a whim," Eli countered sagely. He turned off the engine and patted her hand paternally, once again becoming the father she'd lost, way too young. "I'm not sure what has gone on here, but I know a misunderstanding when I see one, Jacey," he murmured. "Whatever my son meant to say to you, whatever he was trying to accomplish, it's not what he ended up doing. The only question is, what are *you* going to do about it?"

JACEY THOUGHT about what Eli had said, while the two of them did the holiday marketing. By the time she got back to the ranch and put the groceries away, she knew what she had to do. Find Rafferty Evans. Give him a piece of her mind. And see where they went from there....

"He went riding," Gabby said.

Curly added, "He's back now."

"Check the stables," Red advised.

Jacey drew a deep breath and settled the sleeping Caitlin into the Pack 'n Play she kept in the bunkhouse. She tucked the swaddling blanket around her slumbering babe and straightened. "You fellas mind watching Caitlin for me for a few minutes?"

Smiles all around. "Be happy to, Jacey," Curly said.

Red grinned. "You know we love her."

"We love *you*," Stretch emphasized, to a rumble of masculine agreement.

Jacey felt a lump in her throat the size of a walnut. This right here, she thought, was Christmas. Now, if only she could extend that joy….

"I love you fellas, too," she said softly. So much she didn't know what she was going to do if she couldn't be a part of the bunkhouse camaraderie anymore. Figuring it was now or never, she headed for the stables but was thwarted again.

"He went up to the ranch house about fifteen minutes ago. Check there," Hoss told her.

Jacey turned around and marched back to the house.

Eli was doing what he did most afternoons—he was napping on the sofa.

Rafferty was not in the kitchen, living room or study.

Heartbeat accelerating, she headed back to his bedroom. Knocked.

The door opened. Rafferty stood there, newly showered and dripping wet, a towel wrapped around his hips. Jacey swallowed around the sudden dryness of her throat. Fighting the urge to make love to him then and there, she pushed back her desire and strode past him. "I need to talk to you." Ignoring the incredibly sexy way he looked, she shut the door behind her and whirled to face him. Deciding to get to the point, she stated bluntly, "I don't want to leave."

A flicker of happiness crossed his face, then was replaced by an emotion she could not read. His eyes solemn, he returned softly, "I don't want you to leave, either."

Jacey gulped. "I like it here."

His lips curved into a smile. "I like you here."

His teasing sent a spiral of warmth deep inside her. Deliberately, she kept her eyes locked with his. "Then why are you trying to get rid of me?" This much she had to know.

Rafferty looked confused again. "I'm not."

Jacey sighed in frustration and trod a little closer. "Let's refresh. You just found a replacement chef for the ranch, an alternate place for me and my baby to live, and gave me an astounding five-figure check to ease my exit. I'd call that a pretty big hint, big guy."

"Or an opportunity," Rafferty corrected, gently clasping her arms. "I didn't want to be responsible for holding you back. I wanted to help you have everything you ever wanted, careerwise. So you wouldn't look back one day and think you had made a mistake taking a temporary job at the ranch and then never moving on again. I didn't want you to get three years down the road and regret getting off the career path you were on, or neglecting to blaze a new one, just because you were comfortable here."

This was sounding a lot like Mindy, and not at all like Rafferty Evans.

Jacey licked her suddenly dry lips and fought the increasingly self-conscious flush in her cheeks. "And if you weren't trying to help me achieve the dreams I should be seeking, what kind of Christmas gift would you have given me?" she asked curiously.

Without hesitation, Rafferty walked over to his bureau, opened the drawer and took out a velvet jewelry box. Expression sobering all the more, he came back and handed it to her. "This is what I wanted to give you," he said, his voice suddenly hoarse.

Jacey opened it up.

Inside was a platinum diamond engagement ring.

The gift she had been hoping he would present her with, the one that would make all her dreams come true.

"I wanted to ask you to marry me," he continued, threading his hands through her hair and lifting her face up to his. "But then...I overheard you talking to your sister while you were wrapping presents, and realized I wasn't being fair. So I went another direction, hoping that if I sacrificed what I wanted and gave you what you wanted instead, it would all work out in the end." His eyes lasered in on hers. "Hoping you'd know what I realized a long time ago—that we belong together."

Well, at least he got that part right, Jacey thought. "First of all. Opening up my own business one day is a dream, but not one I want to pursue until Caitlin is a lot older. Right now, all I want to do is be on the mommy track, enjoy every moment of her pre-k years and cook for you and the guys. Maybe take some cooking classes now and then so I can really expand my repertoire. Second, and even more important..." Her voice caught a little. She forced herself to go on as she withdrew an envelope from her pocket and handed it to him.

"This was my gift."

He opened it up. Inside was a card with a deliriously dancing Snoopy, and the hand-written note, "I.O.U. unlimited tender loving care—and holiday cheer—from this day forward...."

A smile spread slowly across his face. "There's nothing I want more, especially now that my Ebenezer Scrooge days are over."

Their eyes met and held.

"I'm glad you like your gift."

"I do," he said gruffly.

"So." She cleared her throat. "If this ring is a proposal of marriage—"

"It is." His tone left no doubt about what he wanted.

Tears of bliss filled her eyes. "Then my answer is yes," she replied just as resolutely. "I will marry you."

They pledged their commitment to each other with a long, tender kiss.

Drawing back, Jacey looked deep into his eyes and said the words she had longed to express. "I love you, Rafferty Evans, with all my heart and soul."

His voice turned low and gravelly. He pressed her tightly against him. "I love you, too, Jacey. So much more than words can ever say."

He kissed her again. And again and again. And by the time they had finished, they knew that they were meant to be together.

Not just for now, but forever.

THEIR EXUBERANT MOOD only accelerated as Christmas descended upon them. And when at last Jacey sat down in the bunkhouse to open presents, and she saw what the cowboys had worked so hard to arrange, her heart filled with even more love. "A Global Positioning System for my car!" No wonder they'd had to go all the way to El Paso to have it installed in the dashboard. "Fellas! What a great gift!"

The cowboys grinned from ear to ear. "We don't want you getting lost anymore," Stretch said.

"This way, wherever you are, you'll know how to find your way back to the ranch," Hoss added.

"And don't forget the new stereo system, too, with the six-CD changer," Curly piped in.

"No way I could," Jacey gushed. She shook her head in admiration. "You guys outdid yourself."

Red traced the Lost Mountain Ranch logo on their presents from Rafferty and his dad. "These new sterling-silver belt buckles are pretty fancy, too."

Jacey agreed it had been a particularly thoughtful gift, as well received as the sturdy leather work gloves she'd given all the men.

Gabby winked. "Although, got to admit, the extra-fat bonus checks we got in our Christmas stockings are awfully nice, too."

"What can I say?" Rafferty grinned, spreading as much joy as Santa himself. He wrapped his arm around Jacey, kissing her and the baby in her arms. "Jacey and Caitlin brought me back my holiday spirit."

Epilogue

Six months later…

Jacey and Rafferty faced off in the suite that would soon be her former bedroom at Lost Mountain Ranch. She shook her head at the mischievous glint in her fiancé's eyes, scolded, "I don't think the groom is supposed to see the bride before the wedding."

And he wouldn't have, if her sister hadn't gone off to get baby Caitlin into her white organza wedding-day dress.

Looking resplendent in a dove-gray morning coat and tails, Rafferty held a bit of greenery above her head. "The bride is not supposed to be standing beneath the mistletoe, either."

Jacey flirted back shamelessly. "Especially in June. It's wedding season, Rafferty."

"I know." He regarded her with mock seriousness, even as he wrapped his free arm around her waist and drew her against him. "That's why we're getting married." He chuckled as the petticoats beneath her full skirt swished. "'Tis the season to be jolly and all that…."

Jacey let out a tremulous sigh. "You're incorrigible."

He misbehaved even more. "Your fault."

Feeling like a kid, too, Jacey regarded him with exaggerated reproof. "And how is that, Mr. Evans?"

He kissed her lips gently. "You've given me the Christmas spirit to carry around in my heart all year round, Mrs. Soon-To-Be-Evans."

Thinking to heck with tradition, Jacey wreathed her arms about his neck and kissed him back just as tenderly. "Who would have known…"

"Certainly not me." Rafferty sighed his contentment. They were about to kiss again, when voices sounded on the other side of the bedroom door. They were followed by a knock. His arm still around her waist, Rafferty opened the door. Eli and Mindy stood there, not surprised at all to discover where the groom had happened to end up.

"Honestly," Mindy said as she shifted her niece to her other hip. "Must you two look so deliriously happy all the time?"

"Your sister might start to think you and your daughter belong here," Eli teased.

They all laughed.

Once Mindy had understood how right this was for Jacey, she had been as supportive and happy for her sister as everyone else.

"In any case, we thought you might be sneaking a little wedding cheer," Eli said dryly.

Every bit as poker-faced as his father, Rafferty held the greenery aloft and claimed, "We're testing the mistletoe."

"Then we'll let you have at it," Eli returned, a glint of approval in his faded blue eyes.

Mindy smiled at them fondly, too. "Just not too long. The wedding guests are waiting."

Jacey and Rafferty kissed again. Held each other tight. Finally, they drew apart, knowing it was time. "Ready to go out and make this official?" Rafferty asked.

Never more sure of anything in her life, Jacey nodded.

Hand in hand, they walked out to the lawn, where a sea of white chairs had been set up. With Mindy and Caitlin on one side of them, bearing witness, Eli on the other, Jacey and Rafferty committed to a lifetime of love and bliss. When the minister blessed their union, a cheer went up that echoed through the ranch. In that blissful moment, Jacey knew she and Rafferty had received the best gift of all—they had come home to each other, to love, at long last.

* * * * *

Watch for Cathy Gillen Thacker's next book
in the MADE IN TEXAS miniseries,
FOUND: ONE BABY,
coming in April 2009,
only from Harlequin American Romance!

Silhouette Desire kicks off 2009 with
MAN OF THE MONTH,
a yearlong program featuring
incredible heroes by stellar authors.

When navy SEAL Hunter Cabot returns home for some
much-needed R & R, he discovers he's a married man.
There's just one problem: he's never met his "bride."

Enjoy this sneak peek at Maureen Child's
AN OFFICER AND A MILLIONAIRE.
Available January 2009 from Silhouette Desire.

One

Hunter Cabot, Navy SEAL, had a healing bullet wound in his side, thirty days' leave and, apparently, a wife he'd never met.

On the drive into his hometown of Springville, California, he stopped for gas at Charlie Evans's service station. That's where the trouble started.

"Hunter! Man, it's good to see you! Margie didn't tell us you were coming home."

"Margie?" Hunter leaned back against the front fender of his black pickup truck and winced as his side gave a small twinge of pain. Silently then, he watched as the man he'd known since high school filled his tank.

Charlie grinned, shook his head and pumped gas. "Guess your wife was lookin' for a little 'alone' time with you, huh?"

"My—" Hunter couldn't even say the word. *Wife?* He didn't have a wife. "Look, Charlie..."

"Don't blame her, of course," his friend said with a wink

as he finished up and put the gas cap back on. "You being gone all the time with the SEALs must be hard on the ol' love life."

He'd never had any complaints, Hunter thought, frowning at the man still talking a mile a minute. "What're you—"

"Bet Margie's anxious to see you. She told us all about that R and R trip you two took to Bali." Charlie's dark brown eyebrows lifted and wiggled.

"Charlie..."

"Hey, it's okay, you don't have to say a thing, man."

What the hell could he say? Hunter shook his head, paid for his gas and as he left, told himself Charlie was just losing it. Maybe the guy had been smelling gas fumes too long.

But as it turned out, it wasn't just Charlie. Stopped at a red light on Main Street, Hunter glanced out his window to smile at Mrs. Harker, his second-grade teacher who was now at least a hundred years old. In the middle of the crosswalk, the old lady stopped and shouted, "Hunter Cabot, you've got yourself a wonderful wife. I hope you appreciate her."

Scowling now, he only nodded at the old woman—the only teacher who'd ever scared the crap out of him. What the hell was going on here? Was everyone but him nuts?

His temper beginning to boil, he put up with a few more comments about his "wife" on the drive through town before finally pulling into the wide, circular drive leading to the Cabot mansion. Hunter didn't have a clue what was going on, but he planned to get to the bottom of it. Fast.

He grabbed his duffel bag, stalked into the house and paid no attention to the housekeeper, who ran at him, fluttering both hands. "Mr. Hunter!"

"Sorry, Sophie," he called out over his shoulder as he took the stairs two at a time. "Need a shower, then we'll talk."

He marched down the long, carpeted hallway to the rooms

that were always kept ready for him. In his suite, Hunter tossed the duffel down and stopped dead. The shower in his bathroom was running. His *wife?*

Anger and curiosity boiled in his gut, creating a churning mass that had him moving forward without even thinking about it. He opened the bathroom door to a wall of steam and the sound of a woman singing—off-key. Margie, no doubt.

Well, if she was his wife...Hunter walked across the room, yanked the shower door open and stared in at a curvy, naked, temptingly wet woman.

She whirled to face him, slapping her arms across her naked body while she gave a short, terrified scream.

Hunter smiled. "Hi, honey. I'm home."

* * * * *

*Be sure to look for
AN OFFICER AND A MILLIONAIRE
by* USA TODAY *bestselling author Maureen Child.
Available January 2009 from Silhouette Desire.*

CELEBRATE
60 YEARS
OF PURE READING PLEASURE
WITH HARLEQUIN®!

We'll be spotlighting a different series
every month throughout 2009
to celebrate our 60th anniversary.
Look for Silhouette Desire® in January!

Collect all 12 books in the Silhouette Desire®
Man of the Month continuity, starting in
January 2009 with *An Officer and a Millionaire*
by *USA TODAY* bestselling author
Maureen Child.

*Look for one new Man of the Month title
every month in 2009!*

Silhouette®

SPECIAL EDITION™

The Bravos meet the Jones Gang
as two of Christine Rimmer's famous
Special Edition families come together
in one very special book.

THE STRANGER
AND TESSA JONES
by
CHRISTINE RIMMER

Snowed in with an amnesiac stranger during a
freak blizzard, Tessa Jones soon finds out her
guest is none other than heartbreaker Ash Bravo.
And that's when things really heat up....

Available January 2009
wherever you buy books.

REQUEST YOUR FREE BOOKS!

2 FREE NOVELS PLUS 2
FREE GIFTS!

Love, Home & Happiness!

YES! Please send me 2 FREE Harlequin® American Romance® novels and my 2 FREE gifts (gifts are worth about $10). After receiving them, if I don't wish to receive any more books, I can return the shipping statement marked "cancel." If I don't cancel, I will receive 4 brand-new novels every month and be billed just $4.24 per book in the U.S. or $4.99 per book in Canada. That's a savings of close to 15% off the cover price! It's quite a bargain! Shipping and handling is just 25¢ per book, along with any applicable taxes.* I understand that accepting the 2 free books and gifts places me under no obligation to buy anything. I can always return a shipment and cancel at any time. Even if I never buy another book from Harlequin, the two free books and gifts are mine to keep forever.

154 HDN EEZK 354 HDN EEZV

Name	(PLEASE PRINT)
Address	Apt. #
City	State/Prov.	Zip/Postal Code

Signature (if under 18, a parent or guardian must sign)

Mail to the **Harlequin Reader Service:**
IN U.S.A.: P.O. Box 1867, Buffalo, NY 14240-1867
IN CANADA: P.O. Box 609, Fort Erie, Ontario L2A 5X3

Not valid to current subscribers of Harlequin® American Romance® books.

Want to try two free books from another line?
Call 1-800-873-8635 or visit www.morefreebooks.com.

* Terms and prices subject to change without notice. N.Y. residents add applicable sales tax. Canadian residents will be charged applicable provincial taxes and GST. Offer not valid in Quebec. This offer is limited to one order per household. All orders subject to approval. Credit or debit balances in a customer's account(s) may be offset by any other outstanding balance owed by or to the customer. Please allow 4 to 6 weeks for delivery. Offer available while quantities last.

Your Privacy: Harlequin is committed to protecting your privacy. Our Privacy Policy is available online at www.eHarlequin.com or upon request from the Reader Service. From time to time we make our lists of customers available to reputable third parties who may have a product or service of interest to you. If you would prefer we not share your name and address, please check here.

HAR08R2

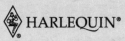

HARLEQUIN®

American ★ Romance®

TINA LEONARD
The Texas
Ranger's Twins

Men Made in America

The promise of a million dollars has lured
Texas Ranger Dane Morgan back to his family
ranch. But he can't be forced into marriage to
single mother of twin girls, Suzy Wintertone,
who is tempting as she is sweet—can he?

Available January 2009
wherever books are sold.

LOVE, HOME & HAPPINESS

www.eHarlequin.com   HAR75245

Home to Texas and straight to the altar!

THE
TEXAS
BROTHERHOOD

Luke: The Cowboy Heir
by
PATRICIA THAYER

Luke never saw himself returning to
Mustang Valley. But as a Randell the land
is in his blood and is calling him back…
And blond beauty Tess Meyers is waiting
for Luke Randell's return….

Available January 2009
wherever you buy books.

SPECIAL EDITION™

USA TODAY bestselling author
MARIE FERRARELLA

FORTUNES OF TEXAS:
RETURN TO RED ROCK

PLAIN JANE AND THE PLAYBOY

To kill time at a New Year's party, playboy
Jorge Mendoza shows the host's teenage son
how to woo the ladies. The random target of
Jorge's charms: wallflower Jane Gilliam. But
with one kiss at midnight, introverted Jane
turns the tables on this would-be Casanova,
as the commitment-phobe falls for her hook,
line and sinker!

*Available January 2009
wherever you buy books.*

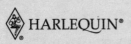

HARLEQUIN®

American ★ Romance®

COMING NEXT MONTH

#1241 THE TEXAS RANGER'S TWINS by Tina Leonard
Men Made in America
Texas Ranger Dane Morgan has been lured home to Union Junction by the prospect of inheriting a million dollars. All he needs to do is live on the Morgan ranch for a year...and marry Suzy Winterstone. While the sassy single mother of toddler twin daughters is as tempting as she is sweet, no Ranger worth his salt can be forced into marriage by a meddling matchmaker! *Can he?*

#1242 MILLION-DOLLAR NANNY by Jacqueline Diamond
Harmony Circle
When her con man ex-fiancé takes off with all her money, Sherry LaSalle finds herself in need of something she's never had before—a job! The socialite may have found her calling, though, as a nanny for Rafe Montoya's adorable twin niece and nephew. The sexy mechanic couldn't be more different than the ex-heiress, but there's something about Sherry that's winning over the kids...and melting Rafe's heart.

#1243 BABY ON BOARD by Lisa Ruff
Baby To Be
Kate Stevens is interviewing daddy candidates. Applicants must be kind, must be stable and must be looking for the same white-picket-fence life Kate has always dreamed of. Unfortunately for her, fun-loving, risk-taking world traveler Patrick Berzani—the baby's biological father—wants to be considered for the position....

#1244 MOMMY IN TRAINING by Shelley Galloway
Motherhood
The arrival of a megastore in Crescent View, Texas, is horrible news for Minnie Clark. Her small boutique is barely making a profit, plus she has the added responsibility of providing for her young niece. So when Minnie discovers that her high-school crush, Matt Madigan, works for the megastore, the new mommy is ready for battle!

www.eHarlequin.com

HARCNMBPA1208